GOD'S GYM

GOD'S GYM

* * *

JOHN EDGAR
WIDEMAN

HOUGHTON MIFFLIN COMPANY

BOSTON • NEW YORK

2005

For information about permission to reproduce selections
from this book, write to Permissions, Houghton Mifflin Company,
215 Park Avenue South, New York, New York 10003.

Visit our Web site: www.houghtonmifflinbooks.com.

Library of Congress Cataloging-in-Publication Data
Wideman, John Edgar.
God's gym / John Edgar Wideman.
p. cm.
Contents: Weight — Hunters — Sharing — The silence of Thelonious
Monk — Are dreams faster than the speed of light — Who invented the
jump shot — What we cannot speak about we must pass over in silence —
Fanon — Who weeps when one of us goes down blues — Sightings.
ISBN 0-618-51525-9
1. United States — Social life and customs — Fiction.
2. African Americans — Fiction. I. Title.
PS3573.I26G29   2005
813'.54 — dc22   2004054071

Book design by Melissa Lotfy

Printed in the United States of America

QUM 10 9 8 7 6 5 4 3 2 1

Some of these stories first appeared, in somewhat different form, in the following
publications: "Weight" in *Callaloo;* "Hunters" in *XConnect* (University of Pennsylvania); "Sharing" in *GQ;* "The Silence of Thelonious Monk" in *Esquire;* "Are
Dreams Faster Than the Speed of Light" in *Playboy;* "Who Invented the Jump
Shot" in *Hoop Roots;* "What We Cannot Speak About We Must Pass Over in Silence" in *Harper's Magazine;* "Fanon" in *The Island;* and "Who Weeps When
One of Us Goes Down Blues" in *Fiction.*

To Catherine with love—
thank you for helping me make these stories

CONTENTS

GOD'S GYM

Weight

M Y MOTHER is a weightlifter. You know what I mean. She understands that the best-laid plans, the sweetest beginnings, have a way of turning to shit. Bad enough when life fattens you up just so it can turn around and gobble you down. Worse for the ones like my mother who life keeps skinny, munching on her daily, one cruel little needle-toothed bite at a time so the meal lasts and lasts. Mom understands life don't play so spends beaucoup time and energy getting ready for the worst. She lifts weights to stay strong. Not barbells or dumb-bells, though most of the folks she deals with, especially her sons, act just that way, like dumbbells. No. The weights she lifts are burdens—her children's, her neighbors, yours. Whatever awful calamities arrive on her doorstep or howl in the news, my mom squeezes her frail body beneath them. Grips, hoists, holds the weight. I swear sometimes I can hear her sinews squeaking and singing under a load of invisible tons.

I ought to know, since I'm one of the burdens bowing her shoulders. She loves heavy, hopeless me unconditionally. Be-fore I was born, Mom loved me, forever and ever till death do us part. I'll never be anyone else's darling, darling boy, so it's her fault, her doing, isn't it, that neither of us can face the thought of losing the other. How could I resist reciprocating her love. Needing her. Draining her. Feeling her straining underneath me, the pop and crackle of her arthritic joints, her gray hair siz-zling with static electricity, the hissing friction, tension, and pressure as she lifts more than she can bear. Bears more than she can possibly lift. You have to see it to believe it. Like the Flying Wallendas or Houdini's spine-chilling escapes. One of the greatest shows on earth.

My mother believes in a god whose goodness would not permit him to inflict more troubles than a person can handle. A god of mercy and salvation. A sweaty, bleeding god presiding over a fitness class in which his chosen few punish their muscles. She should wear a T-shirt: *God's Gym.*

In spite of a son in prison for life, twin girls born dead, a mind-blown son who roams the streets with everything he owns in a shopping cart, a strung-out daughter with a crack baby, a good daughter who miscarried the only child her dry womb ever produced, in spite of me and the rest of my limp-along, near-to-normal siblings and their children — my nephews doping and gangbanging, nieces unwed, underage, dropping babies as regularly as the seasons — in spite of breast cancer, sugar diabetes, hypertension, failing kidneys, emphysema, gout, all resident in her body and epidemic in the community, knocking off one by one her girlhood friends, in spite of corrosive poverty and a neighborhood whose streets are no longer safe even for gray, crippled-up folks like her, my mom loves her god, thanks him for the blessings he bestows, keeps her faith he would not pile on more troubles than she could bear. Praises his name and prays for strength, prays for more weight so it won't fall on those around her less able to bear up.

You've seen those iron-pumping, muscle-bound brothers fresh out the slam who show up at the playground to hoop and don't get picked on a team cause they can't play a lick, not before they did their bit, and sure not now, back on the set, stiff and stone-handed as Frankenstein, but finally some old head goes on and chooses one on his squad because the brother's so huge and scary-looking sitting there with his jaw tight, lip poked out, you don't want him freaking out and kicking everybody's ass just because the poor baby's feelings is hurt, you know what I mean, the kind so buff looks like his coiled-up insides about to bust through his skin or his skin's stripped clean off his body so he's a walking anatomy lesson. Well, that's how my mom looks to me sometimes, her skin peeled away, no secrets, every taut nerve string on display.

I can identify the precise moment when I began to marvel at my mother's prodigious strength, during a trip with her one afternoon to the supermarket on Walnut Street in Shadyside, a Pittsburgh, Pennsylvania, white community with just a few families of us colored sprinkled at the bottom ends of a couple of streets. I was very young, young enough not to believe I'd grow old, just bigger. A cashier lady who seemed to be acquainted with my mother asked very loudly, Is this your son, and Mom smiled in reply to the cashier's astonishment, saying calmly, Yes, he is, and the doughy white lady in her yellow Krogers smock with her name on the breast tried to match my mother's smile but only managed a fake grin like she'd just discovered shit stinks but didn't want anybody else to know she knew. Then she blurted, He's a tall one, isn't he.

Not a particularly unusual moment as we unloaded our shopping cart and waited for the bad news to ring up on the register. The three of us understood, in spite of the cashier's quick shuffle, what had seized her attention. In public situations the sight of my pale, Caucasian-featured mother and her variously colored kids disconcerted strangers. They gulped. Stared. Muttered insults. We were visible proof somebody was sneaking around after dark, breaking the apartheid rule, messy mulatto exceptions to the rule, trailing behind a woman who could be white.

Nothing special about the scene in Krogers. Just an ugly moment temporarily reprieved from turning uglier by the cashier's remark, which attributed her surprise to a discrepancy in height, not color. But the exchange alerted me to a startling fact — I was taller than my mother. The brown boy, me, could look down at the crown of his light-skinned mother's head. Obsessed by size, like most adolescent boys, size in general and the size of each and every particular part of my body and how mine compared to others, I was always busily measuring and keeping score, but somehow I'd lost track of my mother's size, and mine relative to hers. Maybe because she was beyond size. If someone had asked me my mother's height or weight, I probably would have replied, *Huh. Ubiquitous,* I might say now. A tiny skin-and-bone woman way too huge for size to pin down.

The moment in Krogers is also when I began to marvel at my mother's strength. Unaccountably, unbeknown to me, my body had grown larger than hers, yes, and the news was great in a way, but more striking and not so comforting was the fact that, never mind my advantage in size, I felt hopelessly weak standing there beside my mom in Krogers. A wimpy shadow next to her solid flesh and bones. I couldn't support for one hot minute a fraction of the weight she bore on her shoulders twenty-four hours a day. The weight of the cashier's big-mouthed disbelief. The weight of hating the pudgy white woman forever because she tried to steal my mother from me. The weight of cooking and cleaning and making do with no money, the weight of fighting and loving us iron-headed, ungrateful brats. Would I always feel puny and inadequate when I looked up at the giant fist hovering over our family, the fist of God or the Devil, ready to squash us like bugs if my mother wasn't always on duty, spreading herself thin as an umbrella over our heads, her bones its steel ribs keeping the sky from falling.

Reaching down for the brass handle of this box I must lift to my shoulder, I need the gripping strength of my mother's knobby-knuckled fingers, her superhero power to bear impossible weight.

Since I was reading her this story over the phone (I called it a story but Mom knew better), I stopped at the end of the paragraph above that you just completed, if you read that far, stopped because the call was long distance, daytime rates, and also because the rest had yet to be written. I could tell by her silence she was not pleased. Her negative reaction didn't surprise me. Plenty in the piece I didn't like either. Raw, stuttering stuff I intended to improve in subsequent drafts, but before revising and trying to complete it, I needed her blessing.

Mom's always been my best critic. I depend on her honesty. She tells the truth yet never affects the holier-than-thou superiority of some people who believe they occupy the high ground and let you know in no uncertain terms that you nor nobody else like you ain't hardly coming close. Huh-uh. My mother smiles as often as she groans or scolds when she hears gossip about somebody behaving badly. *My, my, my,* she'll say, and nod and smile and gently broom you, the sinner, and herself into the same crowded heap, no one any better than they should be, could be, absolute equals in a mellow sputter of laughter she sometimes can't suppress, hiding it, muffling it with her fist over her mouth, nodding, remembering how people's badness can be too good to be true, *My, my, my.*

Well, my story didn't tease out a hint of laugh, and forget the 550 miles separating us, I could tell she wasn't smiling either. Why was she holding back the sunshine that could forgive the worst foolishness. Absolve my sins. Retrieve me from the dead-end corners into which I paint myself. Mama, please. Please, please, please, don't you weep. And tell ole Martha not to moan. Don't leave me drowning like Willie Boy in the deep blue sea. Smile, Mom. Laugh. Send that healing warmth through the wire and save poor me.

Was it the weightlifting joke, Mom. Maybe you didn't think it was funny.

Sorry. Tell the truth, I didn't see nothing humorous about any of it. *God's T-shirt.* You know better. Ought to be ashamed of yourself. Taking the Lord's name in vain.

Where do you get such ideas, boy. I think I know my children. God knows I should by now, shouldn't I. How am I not supposed to know you-all after all you've put me through beating my brains out to get through to you. *Yes, yes, yes.* Then one you-all goes and does something terrible I never would have guessed was in you. Won't say you break my heart. Heart's been broke too many times. In so many little itty-bitty pieces can't break down no more, but you-all sure ain't finished with me, are you. Still got some new trick in you to lay on your weary mother before she leaves here.

Guess I ought to be grateful to God an old fool like me's still around to be tricked. Weightlifter. Well, it's different. Nobody ain't called me nothing like weightlifter before. It's different, sure enough.

Now here's where she should have laughed. She'd picked up the stone I'd bull's-eyed right into the middle of her wrinkled brow, between her tender, brown, all-seeing eyes, lifted it and turned it over in her hands like a jeweler with a tiny telescope strapped to his skull inspecting a jewel, testing its heft and brilliance, the marks of God's hands, God's will, the hidden truths sparkling in its depths, multiplied, splintered through mirroring facets. After such a brow-scrunching examination, isn't it time to smile. Kiss and make up. Wasn't that Mom's way. Wasn't that how she handled the things that hurt us and hurt her. Didn't she ease the pain of our worst injuries with the balm of her everything's-going-to-be-all-right-in-the-morning smile. The smile that takes the weight, every hurtful ounce, and forgives, the smile licking our wounds so they scab over and she can pick them off our skin, stuff their lead weight into the bulging sack of all sorrows slung across her back.

The possibility that my wannabe story had actually hurt her dawned on me. Or should I say bopped me upside my head like the Br'er Bear club my middle brother loads in his cart to discourage bandits. I wished I was sitting at the kitchen table across from her so I could check for damage, her first, then check myself in the mirror of those soft, brown, incredibly loving mother's eyes. If I'd hurt her even a teeny-tiny bit, I'd be broken forever unless those eyes repaired me. Yet even as I regretted reading her the clumsy passage and prepared myself to surrender wholly, happily to the hounds of hell if I'd harmed one hair on her frail gray head, I couldn't deny a sneaky, smarting tingle of satisfaction at the thought that maybe, maybe words I'd written had touched another human being, mama mia or not.

Smile, Mom. It's just a story. Just a start. I know it needs more work. You were supposed to smile at the weightlifting part.

God not something to joke about.

C'mon, Mom. How many times have I heard Reverend Fitch cracking you up with his corny God jokes.

Time and a place.

Maybe stories are my time and place, Mom. You know. My time and place to say things I need to say.

No matter how bad it comes out sounding, right. No matter you make a joke of your poor mother . . .

Poor mother's suffering. You were going to say, *Poor mother's suffering*, weren't you.

You heard what I said.

And heard what you didn't say. I hear those words too. The unsaid ones, Mom. Louder sometimes. Drowning out what gets said, Mom.

Whoa. We gon let it all hang out this morning, ain't we, son. First that story. Now you accusing me of *your* favorite trick, that muttering under your breath. Testing me this morning, aren't you. What makes you think a sane person would ever pray for more weight. Ain't those the words you put in my mouth. More weight.

And the building shook. The earth rumbled. More weight

descended like God's fist on his Hebrew children. Like in Lamentations. The book in the Bible. The movie based on the book based on what else, the legend of my mother's long-suffering back.

Because she had a point.

People with no children can be cruel. Had I heard it first from Oprah, the diva of suffering my mother could have become if she'd pursued show biz instead of weightlifting. Or was the damning phrase a line from one of Gwen Brooks's abortion blues. Whatever their source, the words fit, and I was ashamed. I do know better. A bachelor and nobody's daddy, but still my words have weight. Like sticks and stones, words can break bones. Metaphors can pull you apart and put you back together all wrong. I know what you mean, Mom. My entire life I've had to listen to people trying to tell me I'm just a white man in a dark skin.

Give me a metaphor long enough and I'll move the earth. Somebody famous said it. Or said something like that. And everybody, famous or not, knows words sting. Words change things. Step on a crack, break your mother's back.

On the other hand, Mom, metaphor's just my way of trying to say two things, be in two places at once. Saying goodbye and hello and goodbye. Many things, many places at once. You know, like James Cleveland singing our favorite gospel tune, "I Stood on the Banks of the Jordan." Metaphors are very short songs. Mini-mini-stories. Rivers between, like the Jordan where ships sail on, sail on and you stand and wave goodbye-hello, hello-goodbye.

Weightlifter just a word, just play. I was only teasing, Mom. I didn't mean to upset you. I certainly intended no harm. I'd swallow every stick of dynamite it takes to pay for a Nobel prize before I'd accept one if it cost just one of your soft, curly hairs.

Smile. Let's begin again.

◆ ◆ ◆

It's snowing in Massachusetts / The ground's white in O-hi-o. Yes, it's snowing in Massachusetts / And ground's white in O-hi-o. Shut my eyes, Mr. Weatherman / Can't stand to see my baby go.

When I called you last Thursday evening and didn't get an answer I started worrying. I didn't know why. We'd talked Tuesday and you sounded fine. Better than fine. A lift and lilt in your voice. After I hung up the phone Tuesday, said to myself, Mom's in good shape. Beat-up but her spirit's strong. Said those very words to myself more than once Tuesday. *Beat-up but her spirit's strong.* The perkiness I sensed in you helped make my Wednesday super. Early rise. Straight to my desk. Two pages before noon and you know me, Mom. Two pages can take a week, a month. I've had two-page years. I've had decades dreaming the one perfect page I never got around to writing. Thursday morning reams of routine and no pages but not to worry, I told myself. After Wednesday's productivity, wasn't I entitled to some down time. Just sat at my desk, pleased as punch with myself till I got bored feeling so good and started a nice novel, *Call It Sleep.* Dinner at KFC buffet. Must have balled up fifty napkins trying to keep my chin decent. Then home to call you before I snuggled up again with the little Jewish boy, his mama, and their troubles in old NYC.

Let your phone ring and ring. Too late for you to be out unless you had a special occasion. And you always let me know well ahead of time when something special coming up. I tried calling a half-hour later and again twenty minutes after that. By then nearly nine, close to your bedtime. I was getting really worried now. Couldn't figure where you might be. Nine-fifteen and still no answer, no clue what was going on.

Called Sis. Called Aunt Chloe. Nobody knew where you were. Chloe said she'd talked with you earlier, just like every other morning. Sis said you called her at work after she got back from lunch. Both of them said you sounded fine. Chloe said you'd probably fallen asleep in your recliner and left the phone in the bedroom or bathroom and your hearing's to the point you can be wide awake but if the TV's on and the phone's not beside you or the ringer's not turned to high, she said sometimes she has to ring and hang up, ring and hang up two, three times before she catches you.

Chloe promised to keep calling every few minutes till she reached you. Said, They have a prayer meeting Thursdays in your mother's building and she's been saying she wants to go and I bet she's there, honey. She's all right, honey. Don't worry yourself, okay. We're old and fuddle-headed now, but we're tough old birds. Your mother's fine. I'll tell her to call you soon's I get through to her. Your mom's okay, baby. God keeps an eye on us.

You know Aunt Chloe. She's your sister. Five hundred miles away and I could hear her squeezing her large self through the telephone line, see her pillow arms reaching for the weight before it comes down on me.

Why would you want to hear any of this. You know what happened. Where you were. You know how it all turned out.

You don't need to listen to my conversation with Sis. Dialing her back after we'd been disconnected. The first time in my life I think my sister ever phoned me later than ten o'clock at night. First time a lightning bolt ever disconnected us. Ever disconnected me from anybody ever.

Did you see Eva Wallace first, Mom, coming through your door, or was it the busybody super you've never liked since you moved in. Something about the way she speaks to her granddaughter, you said. Little girl's around the building all day because her mother's either in the street or the slam and the father takes the child so rarely he might as well live in Timbuktu so you know the super doesn't have it easy and on a couple of occasions you've offered to keep the granddaughter when the super needs both hands and her mind free for an hour. You don't hold the way she busies up in everybody's business or the fact the child has to look out for herself too many hours in the day against the super, and you're sure she loves her granddaughter, you said, but the short way she talks sometimes to a child that young just not right.

Who'd you see first pushing open your door. Eva said you didn't show up after you said you'd stop by for her. She waited a while, she said, then phoned you and got no answer and then a friend called her and they got to running their mouths and Eva said she didn't think again about you not showing up when you were supposed to until she hung up the phone. And not right away then. Said as soon as she missed you, soon as she remembered you-all had planned on attending the Thursday prayer meeting together, she got scared. She knows how dependable you are. Even though it was late, close to your bedtime, she called you anyway and let the phone ring and ring. Way after nine by then. Pulled her coat on over her housedress, scooted down the hall, and knocked on your door cause where else you going to be. No answer so she hustled back to her place and phoned downstairs for the super and they both pounded on your door till the super said, We better have a look just in case, and unlocked your apartment. Stood there staring after she turned the key, trying to see through the door, then slid it open a little and both of them, Eva said, tiptoeing in like a couple of fools after all that pounding and hollering in the hall. Said she never thought about it at the time but later, after everything over and she drops down on her couch to have that cigarette she knew she shouldn't have with her lungs rotten as they are and hadn't smoked one for more than a year but sneaks the Camel she'd been saving out its hiding place in a baggie in the freezer and sinks back in the cushions and lights up, real tired, real shook up and teary, she said, but couldn't help smiling at herself when she remembered all that hollering and pounding and then tipping in like a thief.

It might have happened that way. Being right or wrong

about what happened is less important sometimes than finding a good way to tell it. What's anybody want to hear anyway. Not the truth people want. No-no-no. People want the best-told story, the lie that entertains and turns them on. No question about it, is there. What people want. What gets people's attention. What sells soap. Why else do the biggest, most barefaced liars rule the world.

Hard to be a mother, isn't it, Mom. I can't pretend to be yours, not even a couple minutes' worth before I go to pieces. I try to imagine a cradle with you lying inside, cute, miniature bedding tucked around the tiny doll of you. I can almost picture you asleep in it, snuggled up, your eyes shut, maybe your thumb in your mouth, but then you cry out in the night, you need me to stop whatever I'm doing and rush in and scoop you up and press you to my bosom, lullaby you back to sleep. I couldn't manage it. Not the easy duty I'm imagining, let alone you bucking and wheezing and snot, piss, vomit, shit, blood, you hot and throbbing with fever, steaming in my hands like the heart ripped fresh from some poor soul's chest.

Too much weight. Too much discrepancy in size. As big a boy as I've grown to be, I can't lift you.

Will you forgive me if I cheat, Mom. Dark-suited, strong men in somber ties and white shirts will lug you out of the church, down the stone steps, launch your gleaming barge into the black river of the Cadillac's bay. My brothers won't miss me not handling my share of the weight. How much weight could there be. Tiny, scooped-out you. The tinny, fake wood shell. The entire affair's symbolic. Heavy with meaning, not weight. You know. Like metaphors. Like words interchanged as if they have no weight or too much weight, as if words are never required to bear more than they can stand. As if words, when we're finished mucking with them, go back to just being words.

The word *trouble*. The word *sorrow*. The word *by-and-by*.

I was wrong and you were right, as usual, Mom. So smile.

Certain situations, yours for instance, being a mother, suffering what mothers suffer, why would anyone want to laugh at that. Who could stand in your shoes a heartbeat—*shoes, shoes, everybody got to have shoes*—bear your burdens one instant and think it's funny. Who ever said it's OK to lie and kill as long as it makes a good story.

Smile. Admit you knew from the start it would come to this. Me trembling, needing your strength. It has, Mom, so please, please, a little-bitty grin of satisfaction. They say curiosity kills the cat and satisfaction brings it back. Smiling. Smile, Mom. Come back. You know I've always hated spinach but please spoonfeed me a canful so those Popeye muscles pop in my arms. I meant shapeshifter, not weightlifter. I meant the point of this round, spinning-top earth must rest somewhere, on something or someone. I meant you are my sunshine. My only sunshine.

The problem never was the word *weightlifter,* was it. If you'd been insulted by my choice of metaphor, you would have let me know, not by silence but by nailing me with a quick, funny, signifying dig, and then you would have smiled or laughed and we'd have gone on to the next thing. What must have bothered you, stunned you, was what I said into the phone before I began reading. Said this is about a man scared he won't survive his mother's passing.

That's what upset you, wasn't it. Saying goodbye to you. Practicing for your death in a story. Trying on for size a world without you. Ignoring, like I did when I was a boy, your size. Saying aloud terrible words with no power over us as long as we don't speak them.

So when you heard me let the cat out the bag, you were shocked, weren't you. Speechless. Smileless. What could you say. The damage had been done. I heard it in your first words after you got back your voice. And me knowing your lifelong, deathly fear of cats. Like the big, furry orange tom you told me about, how it curled up on the porch just outside your door, trapping you a whole August afternoon inside the hotbox shanty in Washington, D.C., when I lived in your belly.

Why would I write a story that risks your life. Puts our business in the street. I'm the oldest child, supposed to be the man of the family now. No wonder you cried, Oh Father. Oh Son. Oh Holy Ghost. Why hast thou forsaken me. I know you didn't cry that. You aren't Miss Oprah. But I sure did mess up, didn't I. Didn't I, Mom. Up to my old tricks. Crawling up inside you. My weight twisting you all out of shape.

I asked you once about the red sailor cap hanging on the wall inside your front door. Knew it was my brother's cap on the nail, but why that particular hat, I asked, and not another of his countless fly sombreros on display. Rob, Rob, man of many lids. For twenty years in the old house, now in your apartment, the hat a shrine no one allowed to touch. You never said it, but everybody understood the red hat your good-luck charm, your mojo for making sure Rob would get out the slam one day and come bopping through the door, pluck the hat from the wall, and pull it down over his bean head. Do you remember me asking why the sailor cap. You probably guessed I was fishing. Really didn't matter which cap, did it. Point was you chose the red one and why must always be your secret. You could have made up a nice story to explain why the red sailor cap wound up on the nail and I would have listened as I always listened, all ears, but you knew part of me would be trying to peek through the words at your secret. Always a chance you might slip up and reveal too much. So the hat story and plenty others never told. The old folks had taught you that telling another person your secret wish strips it of its power, a wish's small, small chance, as long as it isn't spoken, to influence what might happen next in the world. You'd never tell anyone the words sheltered in the shadow of your heart. Still, I asked about the red sailor cap because I needed to understand your faith, your weightlifting power, how you can believe a hat, any fucking kind of hat, could bring my baby brother home safe and sound from prison. I needed to spy and pry. Wiretap the telephone in your bosom. Hear the words you would never say to another soul, not even on pain of death.

How would such unsaid words sound, what would they look like on a page. And if you had uttered them, surrendered your stake in them, forfeited their meager, silent claim to work miracles, would it have been worth the risk, even worth the loss, to finally hear the world around you cracking, collapsing, changing as you spoke your little secret tale.

Would you have risen an inch or two from this cold ground. Would you have breathed easier after releasing the heaviness of silent words hoarded so unbearably, unspeakably long. Let go, Mom. Shed the weight just once.

Not possible for you, I know. It would be cheating, I know. The man of unbending faith did not say to the hooded inquisitors piling a crushing load of stones on his chest, *More light. More light.* No. I'm getting my quotes mixed up again. Just at the point the monks thought they'd broken his will, just as spiraling fractures started splintering his bones, he cried, *More bricks. More bricks.*

I was scared, Mom. Scared every cotton-picking day of my life I'd lose you. The fear a singsong taunt like tinnitus ringing in my ear. No wonder I'm a little crazy. But don't get me wrong. Not your fault. I don't blame you for my morbid fears, my unhappiness. It's just that I should have confessed sooner, long, long ago, the size of my fear of losing you. I wish you'd heard me say the words. How fear made me keep my distance, hide how much I depended on your smile. The sunshine of your smiling laughter that could also send me silently screaming out the room in stories I never told you because you'd taught me as you'd been taught, not to say anything aloud I didn't want to come true. Nor say out loud the things I wished to come true.

Doesn't leave a hell of a lot to say, does it. No wonder I'm tongue-tied, scared shitless.

But would it be worth the risk, worth failing, if I could find words to tell our story and also keep us covered inside it, work us invisibly into the fret, the warp and woof of the story's design, safe there, connected there as words in perfect poems, the silver apples of the moon, golden apples of the sun, blue guitars. The two of us like those rhyming pairs *never* and *forever, heart* and *part,* in the doo-wop songs I harmonized with the fellas in the alley around the corner from Henderson's barbershop up on Frankstown Avenue, first me, then lost brother Sonny and his crew, then baby brother Rob and his cut-buddy hoodlums rapping, and now somebody else brown and young and wild and pretty so the song lasts forever and never ever ends even though the voices change back there in the alley where you can hear bones rattling in the men's fists, *fever in the funkhouse looking for a five,* and hear wine bottles exploding and the rusty shopping cart squeaking over the cobblestones of some boy ferrying an old lady's penny-ante groceries home for a nickel once, then a dime, a quarter, four quarters now.

Would it be worth the risk, worth failing.

Shouldn't I try even if I know the strength's not in me. No, you say. Yes. Hold on, let go. Do I hear you saying, Everything's gonna be all right. Saying, Do what you got to do, baby, smiling as I twist my fingers into the brass handle. As I lift.

Hunters

Kap-plow. Crack. Boom. Pow-pow . . . Boom. Boom. Boom. We got 'em. We got 'em. They's down. Both of 'em. Dumb niggers running like they could outrun bullets.

Damn. They sure a mess laying there, ain't they. Got 'em both good.

Lookit the ass on this one. Looks like a woman's ass.

This one's got a big fat nigger butt on him too, and long nappy hair like a girl.

Oh, shit, man. This ass too fine for a man. Shit. I think we shot us a woman. And goddamn. She's still groaning and gurgling. Shit.

Groaning. You sure it's a bitch. Kick 'er over and see.

Don't need to turn her over. Female, all right. And she ain't dead yet.

Well, what you waiting for, boy. Flip the bitch. Yank down them drawers. Cop us some pussy while the ho's still warm.

Man, she's fucked up. Groaning.

What's wrong with you, fool. Why you standing there staring and looking dumb. She be gone in a minute. C'mon. Turn the bitch over. *Uh-uh.* Get the other damned sneaker. Now pull, boy, pull. Pull them jeans clean off.

Owhee. Lookee what we gots here. Some sure-nuff chocolate roundeye. Yessiree. Woolly wench, ain't she. But she's fine, all right. Long, skinny legs. Owwhee. There you go standing looking dumb again. Guess you don't mind cold poontang.

Like mine hot. G'wan now. Move out the way now, boy. You riding sloppy seconds on this one.

And that's how the story starts of what white boys did to my baby. To the only woman I've ever truly loved. Now you'd think from what you've read so far, I'd be mad at them, the white guys. The hunters who came upon us innocently macking in a meadow and shots rang out and we took off running like startled deer for the trees. Weird thing is, though, I'm madder at her than at them. She swears none of them raped her. None even tried. Says nobody ever got rough with her. Which means, as I see it, nobody's fault but hers for giving the booty up. Why should I be mad at white guys. Every time she got down with one of them she was doing what she chose to do. In a way. Or so she says.

Maybe we better go back before the beginning. Back before the nasty scene above that always makes me unhappy, makes me, if truth be told, cry. Back before the woodland slaughter. Before the barking rifles and slobbering *Deliverance* goons.

She was born Jill Jones. As if her name her fate, Jill curtsied and churched and niced her way into the light-skin Jack and Jill social set. A prize Jill in spite of a little extra dark in her velvet skin. No, my Jill's not light and bright nor possesses blow hair, you know, as in blowing in the wind in the back seat of a sky-blue drop-top Chevy blow-blown-blowing past, chicks stuffed in the back seat, laughing, squealing, waving bye-bye all pearly teeth, tans with blue eyes to match the car's color, their blond manes whipped by the wind on their way to the beach. Not Jill. The beach presented problems for my girl's grade of hair. It would sneak home before Jill did if she dunked her sweet cinnamon-doughnut body in the sea. Thus colorful scarves, various experimental cuts, wigs, chemical aids, prayers, and cute hats. *Owwhee.* Her pale girlfriends shouted once when *oh my god* Jill's hair, drenched in a sudden shower, became a nappy storm all over her head. Jill confided to me that she'd wished for a nest of coiling, hissing vipers atop her skull, wished she could flash Medusa's glare, turn to stone the silly, wide-eyed looks, the innocent, knife-edged questions, nervous titters, the pity and stage-whispered asides: Did you see Jill. Wow. What happened to her hair. Talk about a bad hair day. Wow. Are you okay, Jill.

Our hair's better than theirs, Jill once asserted, with what I hoped was conviction. In fact it's finer, more delicate hair than theirs, a fact scientifically confirmed, she declared. Finer follicles. More flexible. Hollow or curved or something, she said, combing her hair out, the first of many hours preparing it for work the next week. The reason why, she said, I couldn't sleep over at her place Sunday night. I hate doing it, I look a wreck, Jill said. Why would I want you here the whole time gawking, spying. Hours to twist it. See you next weekend, okay. And oh how I yearned to grab a big handful of her bushy cotton candy, the soft shield she'd raised between us. More hair than I would have ever guessed she owned. A beautiful morphing mystery and I wanted my nose in it. My fingers and toes. Would drink it. Or wade in it. Baby, ohhh, baby. So beautiful. Brown and comely. Ethiop's star-dusted daughter. Hair the mysterious and fine-stranded texture of ancient perfumed Arabian nights. Let me touch it. Wash it. Towel it dry. Kiss it. Let me lie on its fluffy pillow. Slobber in it while we sleep. I should have begged for a fistful, for one long, lithesome reed of it. She could have easily spared either. As easily as she could have said yes, of course, spend the night. Pounds of fine-spun Egyptian cotton crowning her regal forehead. Framing her dark eyes, her African lips and nose and cheekbones rendered Somali style, full, delicate, chiseled.

In a story I read recently, author had to be a sister cause the hair business runs all through the piece as it often does in sisters' stories, good hair, bad hair, poster girl hair, heads destined never to grace nobody's billboard. Lord, girl. What's happened to your hair. Nappy. Kinky. Turbanize it. Bald it. Dread it. Braid. Twist. Cornrow. Afreakanize. Turn the tables. Make them eat their labels. I was intrigued by a scene in the story in which the main character allows her wayward white husband to play with her hair, indulging him with this usually forbidden pleasure because it's the first night of a weekend they've stolen away from their beige children, beige lives, attempting to repair a deep rent in the marriage cloth, the wife going to the max, letting his white hands muck about in the hair his people had set afire and left burning on her skull for centuries, fire and smoke, skanky, nasty ruins smoldering sometimes when she'd rake her fingers through its thickness, the ash, the grease, the evil words and acid rain would sear her flesh, paint black moons under her nails, recall the burning, smelly curling iron, branding iron, her body still chained, writhing, dancing in the kindling naps, the dry straw pyre heaped at her feet she's trying to stomp out, combing, straightening, fighting back the flames consuming her. *Black sheep, black sheep, have you any wool. Yes sir, yes sir. I'm the Queen of Sheba holding a whole hot head full.* Girl what happened to your hair. What you do to yourself, girl. In the story the sister knows better but lies with her head in her husband's lap anyway, dreaming of a different life she knows won't happen, even as she settles her cheek against his thigh, even as she submits to his curious, loving strokes and rubs and fingerings and quiet awe and perhaps even rapture like a blond, glassy-eyed, tummyful Gerber baby-food baby sucking its thumb, she knows they've lost their chance and this last desperate forty-eight hours or so won't alter a thousand years of failing, failing, but she allows him to play on anyway in her soft acres of hair, her woolly mammoth bush, girl, untouched, natural like Allah or Buddha borned her with, girl, ain't nothing but a party up there and I'd prove it to Jill if she'd let me dig in, spelunk, deep-sea dive, strum the thinner, rounder, hollower, whatever strands like a lute and chant their praises.

But like the dying marriage I read about in the sister's story, it was not to be. *It* in this instance being the project I imagined in my nappy head of saving Jill from herself, salvaging from the ruins and handing her on a platter my own strayed, lost and found head, the head returning home from its long wilderness of chasing what I couldn't have, shouldn't have, didn't need, tan blond girls and black brown girls who tried their best to make me forget what they were or weren't, I forget which way it was supposed to go, we were all confused back then, weren't we baby, we all needed to be counseled, hipped, switch partners, forsake and reclaim our innocence, have certain matters — fears, inadequacies, lies, paradoxes — lobotomized as I hoped to do for you, Jill, offering my funny valentine bloody head on a platter I presented as a heartfelt gift after you'd danced for me naked to a slow-drag Coltrane blues and I'd nearly died I was so happy. So I presented you my head — what's a little talking head between friends — in my solitude, my gratitude, baby, I said I love you just as you are, as you've always been, you are perfect who you are, brown and kinky-headed, tender-headed just like my tender, preachy head on a dish I wish was a silver platter, babe. As if words could restore peace, as if I could extinguish a fire burning for centuries and simultaneously with shout and chant rekindle what had waned between us. Let me touch your hair. Kiss it. Bundle it in a spirit bundle and weigh its incalculable wealth on the scientific scale I hold in my hands, my battered body parts barely functioning on autopilot, Sweet, cause you stole my heart and blew my mind, but here's what's left of my head, the wide eyes, thick lips plastered too high above my chin, my big nose wide open for you, babe. Please, please, please, don't go, girl, don't take my love away, just one more chorus. Encore the part of your naked dance where you sorta collapse or rather get down, *down,* loosen everything you own, giving it up, giving it all up and sinking, flowing down slinky to the floor onto your back and elbow, then roll, coil, twist like the sacred python rubbing the earth's rich life-giving juices into your gloriously colored, speckled skin, the part like one strand of hair bonding, braiding with others till your dance thickens and rises again royally, like Nefertiti's snake-twined crown above her bronze forehead.

It didn't work, did it. You didn't dance for me with your clothes off ever again. Damage done to you too deep to be undone by words, wishes. You never had a chance. Is that hopelessness part of what I love in you. No chance from the jump, even though you excelled in those areas where everybody expected not to see you represented, didn't count on you being present, let alone deserving of praise. My Jill outstanding at math. Blew tuba in the all-city orchestra. Captain of the county champs, undefeated debating team of her 97-percent-white suburban high school. You aspired to become an astronaut, didn't you. Took flying lessons, I bet. As skilled at aeronautics as aerobics. Earned an AAU Junior Olympic bronze medal swimming the 1500 meters, in spite of denser bones and less buoyancy than your pale opponents, in spite of banks of fast-twitch muscles and minimal slow-twitch, you overcame the biological burdens of African descent predisposing you to sprints and attention deficits and dooming poor me to quick starts, rapid acceleration, early burnout, premature ejaculation some whispered when they weren't dissing my slower, reptilian brain's brawn, how its muscles retarded mental activity, rendering me sluggish and thuggish, intent they said on one and only one thing, my one-track mind chasing beasty, fleshy pleasure, you know, what your mom meant when she told you again and again, *Boys are nasty* (read *black* boys). Boys are *only after one thing*. What others, higher up than your mom on the image-making chain, proclaimed and proved by lynching Emmett Till.

But this story's not about black boys, is it. Not my story. It's about Jill, whose early successes weren't enough to allow her to shed her skin. So let's stick to her. Leopards can't change their spots. She simply sank deeper into the miring clay of other people's perceptions in which she played the role of exception to the rule. As perfectly as she performed everything she wasn't spozed to be able to perform, she couldn't alter the rule. Found herself adrift, stranded on a raft, the lonely floating island of her gifts, her achievements, her exceptional status. Jill's teenage heart saddened, began to harden. No room on the stone raft for anybody else.

This movable feast followed her to the best schools. Girls' schools, a women's college, because you can't trust nasty boys. No point placing yourself at risk. Your pussy in harm's way. Because that's how boys see you. Black booty. That's what these cracker college boys (because it's all white boys or almost all in the best schools) thought of you, Jill. A walk on the dark, wild side. Your allegedly weak morals and naturally lascivious inclinations what they see in spite of or maybe because you display time and time again just the opposite of what they expect. You can't escape what their science predicts, what they teach, what you learn about yourself in the best schools.

Let me digress a moment. Our lives, Jill's and mine, parallel each other in numerous particulars. I emphasize the parallel only to remind the reader I know whereof I speak. In a way. Of course there are important differences, too, between Jill and me. Differences, beginning with gender, she's quick to point out, when I presume to know too much about her. As I often do. Anyway, for simplicity's sake and because it's kind of cute and wicked to sustain the Jack and Jill club bourgey riff, let's call me Jack, Jack attending one of the best schools on a hoop scholarship, and here's one difference already, Jack's vita more predictable than Jill's in a way, more a classic pulling himself up by his bootstraps from the slough of the ghetto black Horatio Alger thing, a jock who could read and ace exams and submit without too much fuss to microscopic examination within the glass cage immuring him. Jack, the first of his penniless family, maybe his race, to achieve this or that, Jack who recalls the first

September of his matriculation at an Ivy university, dressed up and in the company of his new white basketball teammates, mostly poor boys themselves also on scholarship, gunfighters all with mile-wide chips on their shoulders *Don't Tread on Me* sauntering coolly into a mixer at College Hall. Turns out what was being *mixed* was Jack's brown body with approximately six hundred white bodies. No contest. He ducked out after three minutes. Belly-flopped on the bed in his dorm room, KOed by the avalanche of whiteness at the threshold of College Hall he had crossed only to save face, his black face he believed maybe his teammates hadn't noticed till that moment at the entrance — mixing.

Ironically, since arriving on campus, he'd been praying to be seen for what he thought he was, just another frosh boll weevil looking for a home. Then all the boys and girls — My God, Jack, what happened to your hair — saw him for what they thought he was and the shit got worse after that.

Enough of my story. Jill doubtless endured similar and more. And different too, she reminds me every chance she gets. It wasn't always about race, she says. Which to me means she meant she chose to participate in activities (some of which she may very well have enjoyed) that set her apart, but ideally, if the strategy worked, if she performed successfully in these activities, her choices would also ensconce her firmly in the larger life of the institution — read *white* life or *colorblind* life — the larger life in turn graced, integrated, equal-opportunitied by her presence. Race, then, in a way, would disappear. In my view this strategy also doomed her to hang with white boys. Giving in to any nasty boy, black or white, of course, would be breaking a rule, going against the grain of how Jill'd been raised to respect herself and carry herself and save herself, but wouldn't she be tempted to consider dalliance with a boy not black, if not entirely kosher, still, wouldn't it be a bit more like being different, like earning her wings as herself, an individual, being her own person, on her own terms, one more sign she was not who she was spozed to be. Her choice of not-colored lovers a breaking away, breaking expectations, breaking new ground like long-distance swimming, excelling in calculus, etc. Mixing into the larger life. Race disappearing.

Woe is me. Do you see why it's not them I'm angry with. We should know them by now. Haven't they inscribed their superior biology, their superior culture, their crimes on the record. Their record as indelible as our records they steal and play and play and play over and over again. We know what they think of us. We know what they are capable of doing to us when they psyche themselves into ignoring — for profit or pleasure — their Protestant or Catholic belief systems, their hard-won Judeo-Christian moral and ethical principles. We know how they work us, play us, smother us, integrate us, exhaust us, kill us. Know what they say about our bodies and hair.

We know all this. So why fuss. Why feign surprise when they invite us in for a cup of tea and the rest happens. Why whine after we permit them to enter our heads, our beds. Whose race disappears. Who's the one who belonged to a race in the first place.

What would it mean then, to know what I know and not act on it. Not do to them as they do to me and mine. Would my restraint, my turning another cheek, one of my big round butt cheeks, for instance, mean I'd transcended racism. Freed myself of its coils. The deep self-destruct of race's grasp.

I don't think so.

So there we were one day, a beautiful sunny June day, lounging in a grassy meadow where we'd hiked after escaping far from the ugly city on a bus. Just the two of us talking, exchanging stories, cooing, speculating on our miraculous survival, the possibility of Jack and Jill withering away, melting down, and the two of us getting it on in new terms, shit we'd invent as we plowed along, after first burying the hatchet, the nasty past, the hate suspicion jealousy anger at what had conspired to turn us both into so much less than we desired to be, turned us into antagonists in some evil scriptwriter's dumb show, in the perverse theaters of our minds conditioned by unlove of self and each other we'd learned in the best schools, a lesson and discipline passed on to us as the sole means of making it, getting ahead, getting along, surviving, entering the mainstream, transcending race, you know what I'm saying. Rapping in the grass, busy regretting and redefining ourselves, and I admit, yes, maybe I was also hoping maybe Jill might be turned on by our prospects, the lovely summer day, our isolation, our positive vibe, our escape to this primal, sylvan sort of green garden and we'd hug and I'd weave wildflowers into her nappy crown, and eventually, though it wasn't the only thing on my mind, braid flowers as in *Lady Chatterley's Lover* into the cashmere thicket between her chocolate thighs, get down finally to our personal, intimate shortcomings and longcomings, exploring what we might offer each other, do for one another once we'd molted, once we'd discarded if we could the silly skins of Jack and Jill and rebaptized ourselves in Zion's cool, clear, crisp waters, our spirits hungering, loving the chance for a new day like that dawn Coltrane blasted in his solos or hard-pressed Malcolm preached near the end before they wasted him . . .

Kap-plow. Crack. Boom. Pow. Pow. Boom. Boom. Boom.

Forgive me father for telling tales in Babylon's tongue, stories full of Babylon's lies, stories slaying us as surely as we die in Babylon's stories.

Let the curtain descend, the phoenix rise. Let me scoop up our bloody bodies sprawled on the grass. It's only ketchup. It's only my green jealousy and red anger.

Let me blow a whistle and start the scene again. All the players on their feet, whole, cleansed of crimson wounds and burns. Let their eyes be clear, expectant.

And you, love. Forgive the jolt of seeing us undone by my unkind imaginings. Forgive me. Forgive yourself. Let's start again. Let's begin. Let's run.

Sharing

MAYONNAISE. He asked for mayonnaise. You can imagine my surprise, since this was the only real word he'd ever spoken to me. For the first two years, every time we passed on the neighborhood streets, he managed to avoid my eyes. For the next two, there was an occasional nod or wave after both of us had figured out that we were going to be around for the long haul, not like lots of families, who seemed to come and go regularly as the seasons, FOR SALE signs sprouting on lawns each spring, moving vans large as whales docked at the curb or backed up into driveways. Though it seemed that his family, like ours, had settled in for the duration, quiet, minding their own business, business the man had made perfectly clear was nobody else's business, you can imagine my surprise after four years of silence when I hear a knock on my door and it's him and he asks for mayonnaise.

His reluctance to speak in our early encounters had convinced me he didn't like white people. An unwelcoming message in his surly look seemed directed not only at me but at all of us. When I discovered he was married to a white woman, it puzzled me. If he held a grudge against us, why'd he marry her. If he loved his white wife, why would he stay mad at everybody like her.

"Mayonnaise," he said. "I'm sorry to disturb you, ma'am, but could I please borrow a dab of mayonnaise."

I'm thinking, *Mayonnaise?* You've never spoken a real word in the whole four years since you moved here, and now the first real word you say is *mayonnaise*. Well, well. Is that what you've been waiting for? Your mayonnaise to run out?

You say *mayonnaise,* then something about a chicken. And I think, *Chicken?* What's a chicken have to do with mayonnaise? But you aren't asking me to approve or disapprove of whatever goes on in your kitchen. You are asking for mayonnaise, and if something about mayonnaise and chicken inspired you to come to my door and knock, well, so be it. Still, I can't help being curious about what you're up to. Maybe you started a chicken sandwich with lettuce and tomato, then discovered the mayo missing. Not chicken soup. Nobody puts mayo in chicken soup, do they. Perhaps you're preparing a deli tray with cold sliced chicken and need mayonnaise for deviled eggs. No, you didn't say eggs, you said chicken, but mayonnaise is full of eggs, isn't it, either way the chicken comes first, doesn't it. And that dumb thought reminds me that people can't answer the simplest questions, and also that I haven't answered yours.

Then you say, "I can't go to the grocery store. I hate to disturb you, but I just can't make it to the grocery store."

I look at him, perhaps look closely for the first time. When I say closely, I mean I find myself seeing his color at the very moment I realize color is mostly what I've been seeing for four years. Now, I'm not strange about race. I don't think color makes a difference. People are people. In fact, I thought the man was handsome the first time I saw him. I would have responded to him the way I respond to any neighbor and maybe with more enthusiasm since I seldom run into good-looking men, colored or not, around here. But I was put off by his stern expression, his silly game of pretending not to notice me. I'm certain there wasn't anything I did that prevented a polite conversational exchange from starting up. This man has a problem with white people, I figured. The surly look on his face says he doesn't like white people, and I'm sure not going to force myself on him. After one of our stiff mini-meetings and greetings, a snowy, windy day, nobody out but the two of us, I couldn't help asking myself, *If he doesn't like white people, why is he living here in Fairwood, where just about everybody, if you don't count a handful of Asians, is white?* One question leading to others, not many others really, but over the years such questions would arise when I'd see him on the street, and since I continued to pass him quite frequently, I guess there were more than a few questions, even though they weren't exactly burning questions because I just kind of left them alone, took them for granted buzzing around in the silent air between us, just like I took his color for granted till the moment I believed I'd sneaked a peek beneath it.

Today as I look at him in my kitchen I wonder why I've never thought of him eating. Not eating chicken necessarily. Not fried chicken, certainly, not the soul-food cliché of greasy fried chicken. I'm not that kind of person. Not one of those people I really don't appreciate living in our neighborhood. Not thinking anything like those people have in mind when they complain about colored or Negroes or worse. I'm not that kind of person. I raised my children not to hate. But it's strange to look at him, one foot, no, two, three feet inside my door, and realize I've never thought of him in a kitchen, sitting down to a meal with his family. As I study his face, he seems thinner, less dark than I recalled. Then I see from the way he's looking at me, I must be taking too long to answer his request for mayonnaise. His jaw begins to drop. I see him, believe it or not, start to come apart before my eyes.

"I can't stand it," he says. "I just can't go to the grocery store. When I bought the chicken, I thought I would be safe for at least a few days. With food in the house I could stay at home and concentrate on what I needed to do."

He's trembling. This man, this tallish, almost good-looking man who happens to be black, this man standing on the threshold of my kitchen, his hand out for mayonnaise, mumbling something about a chicken, is trembling.

Now, if I could go back and start fresh, I would try to worry less about his plans for my mayo and pay more attention to the special opportunity his sudden appearance at my door offered, the chance to get better acquainted, become true neighbors. I can guess what some of you are thinking. I know what I thought myself—the mayonnaise is going to wind up in an X-rated place, and the man busy down there in that place, mayonnaise his favorite erotic dish, his bushy hair rubbing against my bushy hair and mayonnaise smearing his lips as he laps it from my thighs—but no, this is not that kind of story. This is a different story, but I admit the other video crossed my mind too and made me suspicious of his intentions. I'd been easy, maybe too easy. Here's a strange man who'd paid no attention to my existence for four years and I'd opened my door to him, as if none of his rude behavior had hurt me, and now he's standing just a few feet away, his hand out, making a bizarre request. I don't know him. He doesn't know me. Where is this business going? Where does he want it to go? Where do I want it to go?

Believe me, I'm not the kind of person who makes a big deal out of small things. I'm the sort of individual who responds well to crises. I have three children. They're adults now, and all of you with kids know child-rearing toughens you up. Or kills you. You can't afford to waste your time sweating the small stuff. Real crises come pretty regularly. Demand your attention, demand everything. Leave you feeling very drained, very empty. Emptied of what I'm not sure, because I'm not sure I remember who I was twenty-eight years ago, before marriage and the daily, absolute demand that I pay attention nonstop to other people's needs and forget mine. But I do know that for twenty-eight years, a good portion of them spent in this upscale neighborhood my husband worked very hard and continues to work hard for us to live in, even though he's gone, even though he's moved to a condo in another upscale neighborhood in town with another woman, even though our divorce is well on its way to being consummated and I'm alone now except when the children decide to come or go. During the ups and downs of all those years, I was not the type who cried easily. I don't think I've cried more than twice during the course of these rather trying and miserable divorce proceedings. So I'm not making a big thing out of a small thing when I tell you this large black man standing in my kitchen, his face cracking, the trembling passing through his body, this man scares the pee out of me. What have I gotten myself into? Is he sane? Four years like a ghost in the neighborhood, ignoring me when we pass on the street, and now he comes to my door with an absurd request.

Does he know about the divorce? Has he heard about it from the neighbors? Not likely. How would he hear it from the neighbors? I've seldom seen him speaking to anyone, nor anyone to him. But news travels in strange ways. People share cleaning services. People share exterminators. People share mechanics, and this is, after all, a small community, so he might know. He very well might know. An acquaintance of his might play cards with my husband and have heard the stories. My husband drunk, in one of his sloppy, evil moods, may have told the stories I hate him to tell about me and LSD in college and all that dope we smoked together and those scary situations. And the way he claims he rescued me from one kind of life and brought me here to raise our children in peace and quiet and serenity and changed my life and changed his. What does this man know about those stories? Does he know I'm here in the house alone these days? Is he here because he wants something from me, something that has nothing to do with a jar of unhealthy white gook in the refrigerator he claims is necessary to rescue a chicken?

It's strange how things happen, how people behave. The man asked for mayonnaise. I still haven't said yes or said no. Then I take it upon myself, for some inexplicable reason, given my fear and the oddness of the situation, to offer him something he hasn't requested. "Do you want a glass of water? You seem to be upset about something. May I get you a glass of water? Come in. Sit down, please. Let me get you a glass of water."

Like a child, like one of my children after they'd done something bad, something they were proud of for a while but then started to worry about because it might ruin the good thing I'd become for them, destroy the unspoken understanding that they could ask for anything in the world and I'd give it to them if I could, so they'd get worried and become very quiet, wait for me to tell them what to do next, playing me, little darlings again, wanting to be led by the hand, to be dressed or undressed, told to go off to bed or fetch me a glass of water or drink the glass of water I handed them — that's how the man seemed, like a little kid or a teenager who's gone too far and knows he'd better step back from the brink but doesn't exactly know how.

He shuffles like a zombie across the gleaming Mexican tiles to a chair and sits, head down, waiting for a glass of water.

I fill a glass at the sink and then pour it out. Why am I giving him sink water? There's cold, filtered water in the refrigerator. Embarrassed, hoping he hasn't seen my first impulse, hoping he won't take it the wrong way if he has, I dump out the first glass, open the fridge, push the blue button on the water container, run a fresh glass, and put it in his outstretched hand, a large hand, a trembling hand, a hand that looks pinkish on the inside, brownish on the outside.

"I'm sorry, Mrs. . . ." and then he pauses and I know just why he's pausing. He doesn't know my name. But he shouldn't be embarrassed. I want to say to him, "Don't be embarrassed, I don't remember your name either." But I can't say what I wish I could because I do remember. His last name, at least. So I just look at that two-toned hand and wonder why it's trembling, wonder why he doesn't retract it and hide it but leaves it dangling there until his fingers curl around the water glass. "I'm so sorry, Mrs., Mrs. . . ." I could see the three dots hanging in the air, *dot, dot, dot,* meaning he leaves his sentence unfinished. I see the dots the way you can see quotation marks around words when some people talk or see words in their speech italicized.

"I feel foolish now, ma'am," he says. And I wonder where the *ma'am* is coming from. We must be about the same age. This *ma'am* reminds me of the way the only black man I ever saw inside my parents' house addressed my mother. I was still a little girl and once an old dark man driving a bread truck came to pick up Lucy. To him my mom was *ma'am* and my father *mister* or *sir.* Though I never thought of Lucy as old, I guess she was, but the black man seemed really old, older than my parents, so I didn't understand why he called them *sir* and *ma'am,* and now there's this man. "Ma'am," he says, "I'm sorry, I feel foolish, ma'am, sitting in your kitchen. I don't know you. I don't know you at all. And not only don't I know you, but I can't help myself from saying what I'm about to say. Forgive me, please. I'm imposing on your hospitality, but I have no one else to speak to. My wife's been gone two months now. The first month I was pretty sure she was coming back. Now I know for certain that she's not. I heard it from my mother. My wife and my mother are the best of friends. In fact, I think along with everything else she's taken, my wife intends to steal my mother from me. I can't tell you how cruel that would be. I can't tell you how much I need my mother, particularly now. I won't try to tell you, because I don't know you and I'm feeling more foolish with every word I say. But she's gone, my wife, not my mother yet, my mother probably soon, my wife may be at my mother's now, trying to pry loose the threads that connect me to my mother. Or maybe I'm just angry, maybe I'm being unfair, maybe my wife wouldn't do that to me, even though she would do the worst things to me if she could, because she's so angry.

"Do you know she threw a ham at me? The ham missed, fortunately, and landed on the floor. Well, not exactly on the floor, on my shoe, and it was new and suede. The ham had just come out of the oven. It was hot, quite hot. I was lucky. I saw it coming and sidestepped. I'm an athlete, you know. Or once was an athlete, anyway. Still quick enough to sidestep a flying ham. It landed on my shoe. Maybe it would have been better if it had hit me, because the shoe a mess. A little grease on me, a little grease more or less wouldn't make much difference, but it sure made a difference to that suede shoe. Isn't that a silly story? I guess they're both silly stories, my mother, my shoe, and now that I've started, now that I'm babbling, I don't know what foolish thing's going to come out of my mouth next, so I better stop."

"Please, don't stop. Finish your water. I can tell you're really upset. It's not been an easy time lately for me either. You have no way of knowing, but you're talking to a person whose life may be more like yours than you could ever imagine."

He says, "I hope not. I hope to hell not." And gulps down the glass of water.

"It hasn't been two months, just a little over a month, my husband's been gone. You could say he's been gone for twenty-eight years. I think at least that long. I think the only reason I wouldn't say he's been gone longer than that is because I haven't known him much longer than that, but he may have been gone before I met him, as strange as that sounds."

"I know what you mean," he says. "I know what you mean." And his big eyes with their heavy lids and droopy lashes just about close as he hunkers in the chair. I think he's trying to wish more water into the glass. I think he wants more but is afraid to ask. No wonder he's afraid to ask. He's only asked for one thing since he came into my house, mayonnaise, and hasn't received any yet. A glass of water, yes, a chair, yes, but that's not what he asked for. He asked for mayonnaise to go with his chicken and I'd given him a glass of water. And then he gave me a sad story and then I gave him my sad story back—well, not really, but I started, cut him off before he could finish his sad story. So here we are, two people, two sad stories exchanged, no mayonnaise delivered. A mysterious chicken still lurking somewhere in the background, the daylight seeping through the large windows of the kitchen, the moving trucks going up and down the street, FOR SALE signs everywhere. One will soon be going up on our lawn. Perhaps I could pick up a sign for him. He said something about not liking to go out. He said something about not being able to go to the grocery store. Well, perhaps I could save him some trouble. When I go to the real estate agent, I could get two signs. I think all FOR SALE signs are the same. I think they don't have personalized addresses or names on them. I think one size fits all. So I could grab two and put them in the back of the Volvo and give him either one. Or perhaps hand both to him, because he's a man and he could pound one of them into my front lawn and one into his. And he wouldn't have to drive to the village. But then I remember he hasn't asked for a sign. He's asked for mayonnaise.

"Do you have children?"

"I have two daughters," he says. "They're pretty grown up now. Both away at college. One finishing grad school, the other in her sophomore year at State. I visited them both this past month. After their mother had been away a month and I stopped trying to talk myself into believing she was coming back. Difficult as it was, I knew I had to face them. My wife already had talked to them, of course. I didn't think I could do it. Kara would be okay. I knew she would be okay. Kara's the older one. She understands. I think she loves us equally, my wife and me. She's never taken sides. She's been with us almost from the beginning of the marriage, so she remembers how bad things were from the start. Kara's smart, she knows my wife and I shouldn't be together. She understands she has to love two separate people, not the marriage, not a mother and a father. But Ginger, Ginger came along five years after Kara, and Ginger is a dreamer. She dreams of being like her mother. She dreams of being better than her father. I know why. I can't blame her. She's lived through the worst years. She doesn't know me, except as someone running from her mother, hurting her mother, so she sides with her mother, distrusts me for running, dislikes me for running. She thinks there once was something special in the marriage that should have prevented me from running, something precious I destroyed by running. Of course that's just her dream, it's just her wishful thinking, but who can tell Ginger anything? Who would want to tell anybody not to dream, not to wish, not to think the best of something her parents had tried to build? I'm babbling again, aren't I? Sitting in a stranger's kitchen, babbling. It's come to this. Afraid to leave my house. Afraid to go to the grocery store. Whining to a stranger."

"I may be less a stranger than you think. I don't want to be a stranger. I wanted to speak to you from the beginning. May I ask you a personal question? The very first time I saw you, four years ago, I wanted to speak to you. Why didn't you look at me? Why didn't you return my smile?"

"I don't think I saw your smile. I don't think I was looking very far outside myself in those days when we arrived here. I think I was very busy, very distracted. Maybe I knew it was just a matter of time. Moving to this neighborhood was a desperate act, really. The beginning of the end. Besides which, I'm too vain to wear my glasses and don't see things at more than a few feet's distance very well. I have to keep my eyes focused on the ground, just in front of my feet, so I don't trip over things."

"I thought you were surly. I thought you didn't like white people. I was hurt. I gave up trying to be your friend."

"My friend?"

"Yes, your friend."

"I'm sorry to hear that. That's too bad. I could have used friends. I still could use friends."

"Well, perhaps when all of this is over, perhaps when you get your business straight and mine's straightened out, perhaps we could have a cup of coffee or tea and sit down and talk and have another chance at friendship."

"Friendship?"

"I know you didn't ask for friendship. I keep offering you things you don't ask for. You came for mayonnaise, didn't you? Here, let me get you some. How much mayonnaise do you want? A spoonful? Some in the bottom of a cup? I probably have extra in the pantry. I could give you a whole jar."

"Just a bit will do. It's for chicken salad. I want to make chicken salad. It seems the right thing today. If I could just get myself to start in on fixing chicken salad. You know, doing all the little things you have to do so it turns out right. Dice onions and celery, a red pepper if you have one. Cut the chicken into pieces not too big or too little. Mix in mayo till you get the right consistency. Add spices while you stir. I don't know, you may not be somebody who likes chicken salad, but I do, and I don't mind expending oodles of time preparing it to get it the way I like it, and that seems to be the kind of thing I need to do today."

"Chicken salad. Enough mayonnaise for chicken salad, then."

"That's what I was hoping I could borrow. That's what I was hoping would get me through."

"And me – after I've given you some mayonnaise and you've gone back home to fix your chicken salad, what about me? What's going to get me through my day?"

"I'm sorry. I didn't know you were having difficulties too. If I had known, I wouldn't have bothered you for mayonnaise."

"You're not bothering me. What are friends for, if not sharing? And I hope we're going to be friends. I think mayonnaise is just a beginning."

"I didn't know. I just didn't know."

"What didn't you know?"

"That it would be this hard. I knew I was unhappy. I knew both of us had been unhappy for a long time. Since way before we landed here. When she said she needed to leave home, I decided not to try and stop her. We had to do something about the unhappiness. I thought, *Things can't get worse. Let her go.* But things can get worse. And I think they're going to get even worse than they are now."

"You see, you do need a friend. Here. Here's your mayonnaise."

"Thank you so much. I'll replace this."

"Don't be silly. Just take it, please. It's just a stupid jar of mayonnaise. But you do owe me something in return. You can't just take the mayonnaise and leave. You owe me."

"Owe?"

"Oh, I'm just kidding. You know. Not like you actually owe me anything. I'm just making a little joke. But you could give me something in exchange — you could tell me your first name."

"My name?"

"Yes. And then I'll tell you mine. It's not *ma'am*. Let's trade names and smile at each other and then when the door closes behind you and I'm here alone again, I'll have that pleasant exchange to think about, not just mayonnaise. You don't have to worry about replacing it. I have plenty. That's not what I mean. I mean let's exchange names. I mean let's trade smiles. It's been four years. Far too long."

"I agree. I wish it hadn't taken so long. I wish it weren't too late."

"Too late?"

"Well, I think so."

"What do you mean?"

"I mean, she's gone. There's a big empty house. There are my daughters in other cities. I'm not going to stay here. There's no reason for me to stay. So I don't know about a friendship. I don't know if there'll be time for friendship before I leave."

"You don't understand. I don't mean what you're thinking. That's not what I mean. That's not the kind of friendship I want this to be. I just want us to exchange names, smiles, maybe shake hands, remember each other that way. It's never too late to be nice to each other. You know what I mean. Sure you do. Never too late to be nice. Never. Never. Never."

The Silence of Thelonious Monk

ONE NIGHT years ago in Paris, trying to read myself to sleep, I discovered that Verlaine loved Rimbaud. And in his fashion Rimbaud loved Verlaine. Which led to a hip-hop farce in the rain at a train station. The Gare du Nord, I think. The two poets exchanging angry words. And like flies to buttermilk a crowd attracted to the quarrel, till Verlaine pulls a pistol. People scatter and Rimbaud, wounded before, hollers for a cop. Just about then, at the moment I began mixing up their story with mine, with the little I recall of Verlaine's poetry — *Il pleut dans mon coeur / Comme il pleut sur la ville,* lines I recited to impress you, lifetimes ago, didn't I, the first time we met — just then, with the poets on hold in the silence and rain buffeting the train station's iron roof, I heard the music of Thelonious Monk playing somewhere. So softly it might have been present all along as I read about the sorry-assed ending of the poets' love affair — love offered, tasted, spit out, two people shocked speechless, lurching away like drunks, like sleepwalkers, from the mess they'd made. Monk's music just below my threshold of awareness, scoring the movie I was imagining, a soundtrack inseparable from what the actors were feeling, from what I felt watching them pantomime their melodrama.

Someone plays a Monk record in Paris in the middle of the night many years ago and the scratchy music seeping through ancient boardinghouse walls a kind of silent ground upon which the figure of pitter-pattering rain displays itself, rain in the city, rain Verlaine claimed he could hear echoing in his heart, then background and foreground reverse and Monk the only sound reaching me through night's quiet.

Listening to Monk, I closed the book. Let the star-crossed poets rest in peace. Gave up on sleep. Decided to devote some quality time to feeling sorry for myself. Imagining unhappy ghosts, wondering which sad stories had trailed me across the ocean ready to barge into the space that sleep definitely had no intention of filling. Then you arrived. Silently at first. You playing so faintly in the background it would have taken the surprise of someone whispering your name in my ear to alert me to your presence. But your name once heard, background and foreground switch. I'd have to confess you'd been there all along.

In a way it could end there, in a place as close to silence as silence gets, the moment before silence becomes what it must be next, what's been there the whole time patiently waiting, part of the silence, what makes silence speak always, even when you can't hear it. End with me wanting to tell you everything about Monk, how strange and fitting his piano solo sounded in that foreign place, but you not there to tell it to, so it could/did end, except then as now you lurk in the silence. I can't pretend not to hear you. So I pretend you hear me telling what I need to tell, pretend silence is you listening, your presence confirmed word by word, the ones I say, the unspoken ones I see your lips form, that form you.

Two years before Monk's death, eight years into what the critic and record producer Orrin Keepnews characterized as Monk's "final retreat into total inactivity and seclusion," the following phone conversation between Monk and Keepnews occurred:

Thelonious, are you touching the piano at all these days?
No, I'm not.
Do you want to get back to playing?
No, I don't.

I'm only in town for a few days. Would you like to come and visit, to talk about the old days?

No, I wouldn't.

Silence one of Monk's languages, everything he says laced with it. Silence a thick brogue anybody hears when Monk speaks the other tongues he's mastered. It marks Monk as being from somewhere other than wherever he happens to be, his off-beat accent, the odd way he puts something different in what we expect him to say. An extra something not supposed to be there, or an empty space where something usually is. Like all there is to say but you don't say after you learn in a casual conversation that someone precious is dead you've just been thinking you must get around to calling one day soon and never thought a day might come when you couldn't.

I heard a story from a friend who heard it from Panama Red, a conk-haired, redbone, geechee old-timer who played with Satchmo way back when and he's still on the scene, people say, sounding better and better the older he gets, Panama Red who frequented the deli on Fifty-seventh Street Monk used for kosher.

One morning numerous years ago — story time always approximate, running precisely by grace of the benefit of the doubt — Red said, How you doing, Monk.

Uh-huh, Monk grunts.

Good morning, Mr. Monk. How you do-ink this fine morning, Sammy the butcher calls over his shoulder, busy with a takeout order or whatever it is that keeps his back turned.

If a slice of dead lunch meat spoke, it would be no surprise at all to Sammy compared to how high he'd jump, how many fingers he'd lose in the slicer if the bearish, bearded schwartze in a knitted kufi returned his *Good morning*.

Monk stares at the white man in white apron and white T-shirt behind the white deli counter. At himself in the mirror where the man saw him. At the thin, perfect sheets that buckle off the cold slab of corned beef.

Red holds his just-purchased, neat little white package in his hand and wants to get home and fix him a chopped liver and onion sandwich and have it washed down good with a cold Heineken before his first pupil of the afternoon buzzes, so he's on his way out when he hears Sammy say, Be with you in a moment, Mr. Monk.

Leave that mess you're messing wit alone, nigger, and get me some potato knishes, the story goes, and Panama Red cracking up behind Monk's habit of niggering white black brown red Jew Muslim Christian, the only distinction of color mattering the ivory or ebony keys of his instrument and Thelonious subject to fuck with that difference too, chasing rainbows.

Heard the story on the grapevine, once, twice, and tried to retell it and couldn't get it right and thought about the bird — do you remember it — coo-cooing outside the window just as we both were waking up. In the silence after the bird's song I said Wasn't that a dainty dish to set before the king and you said Don't forget the queen and I said Queen doesn't rhyme with sing and you said It wasn't a blackbird singing outside and I said I thought it was a mourning dove and then the bird started up again trying to repeat itself, trying, trying, but never quite getting it right it seemed. So it tried and tried again as if it had fallen in love with the sound it had heard itself coo once perfectly.

Il pleut dans la ville. Rain in the city. When the rain starts to falling / my love comes tumbling down / and it's raining teardrops in my heart. Rain a dream lots of people are sharing and shyly Monk thinks of how it might feel to climb in naked with everybody under the covers running through green grass in a soft summer shower. Then it's windshield wipers whipping back and forth. Quick glimpses of the invisible city splashing like eggs broken against the glass. I'm speeding along, let's say the West Side Highway, a storm on top, around, and under. It feels like being trapped in one of those automatic car washes doing its best to bust your windows and doors, rapping your metal skin like drumsticks. I'm driving blind and crazed as everybody else down a flooded highway no one with good sense would be out on on a night like this. Then I hit a swatch of absolute quiet under an overpass and for a split second anything is possible. I remember it has happened before, this leap over the edge into vast, unexpected silence, happened before and probably will again if I survive the furious storm, the traffic and tumult waiting to punish me instantly on the far side of the underpass. In that silence that's gone before it gets here good I recalled exactly another time, driving at night with you through a rainstorm. Still in love with you though I hadn't been with you for years, ten, fifteen, till that night of dog-and-cat rain on an expressway circling the city after our eyes had met in a crowded room. You driving, me navigating, searching for a sign to Woodside you warned me would come up all the sudden. There it is. There it is. You shouted. Shit. I missed it. We can get off the next exit, I said. But you said no. Said you didn't know the way. Didn't want to get lost in the scary storm in a scary neighborhood. I missed the turn for your apartment and you said, It's late anyway. Too late to go back and you'd get hopelessly lost coming off the next exit, so we continued downtown to my hotel where you dropped me after a good-night, goodbye-again peck on the cheek. Monk on the radio with a whole orchestra rooty-tooty at town hall, as we raced away from the sign I didn't see till we passed it. Monk's music breaking the silence after we missed our turn, after we hollered to hear each other over the rain, after we flew over the edge and the roof popped off and the sides split and for a moment we were suspended in a soundless bubble where invisible roads crisscrossed going nowhere, anywhere. Airborne, the tires aquaplaning, all four hooves of a galloping horse simultaneously in the air just like Muybridge, your favorite photographer, claimed, but nobody believed the nigger, did they, till he caught it on film.

Picture five or six musicians sitting around Rudy Van Gelder's living room, which is serving as a recording studio this afternoon. Keepnews is paying for the musicians' time, for Van Gelder's know-how and equipment, and everybody ready to record but Monk. Monk's had the charts a week and Keepnews knows he's studied them from comments Monk muttered while the others were sauntering in for the session. But Monk is Monk. He keeps fiddle-faddling with a simple tune, da, da, da, da, plunks the notes, stares into thin air as if he's studying a house of cards he's constructed there, waiting for it to fall apart. Maybe the stare's not long in terms of minutes (unless you're Keepnews, paying the bill) but long enough for the other musicians to be annoyed. Kenny Clark, the drummer, picks up the Sunday funnies from a coffee table. Monk changes pace, back-pedals midphrase, turns the notes into a signifying riff.

K.C., you know you can't read. You drum-drum dummy. Don't be cutting your eyes at me. Ima ABC this tune to death, Mister Kenny Clark. Take my time wit it. Uh-huh. One-and-two and one-and-two it to death, K.C. Don't care if your eyes light up and your stomach says howdy. One anna two anna one anna we don't start till I say start. Till I go over it again. Pick it clean. All the red boogers of meat off the bone then belch and fart and suck little strings I missed out my teefs and chew them last, salty, sweet gristle bits till the cows come home, and then, maybe then it might be time to start so stop bugging me with your bubble eyes like you think you got somewhere better to go.

Once I asked Monk what is this thing called love. Bebop, hip-hop, whatever's good till the last drop and you never get enough of it even when you get as much as you can handle, more than you can handle, he said, just as you'd expect from somebody who's been around such things and appreciates them connoisseurly but also with a passionate innocence so it's always the first time, the only time love's ever happened and Monk can't help but grunt uh-huh, uh-huh while he's playing even though he's been loved before and it ain't no big thing, just the only thing, the music, love, lifting me.

Monk says he thinks of narrow pantherish hips, the goateed

gate to heaven, and stately, stately he slides the silky drawers down, pulls them over her steepled knees, her purple-painted toes. Tosses the panties high behind his back without looking because he knows Pippen's where he's supposed to be, trailing the play, sniffing the alley-oop dish, already slamming it through the hoop so Monk can devote full attention to sliding both his large, buoyant hands up under the curve of her buttocks. A beard down there trimmed neat as Monk trims his.

Trim, one of love's names. Poontang. Leg. Nooky. Cock.

Next chorus also about love. Not so much a matter of mourning a lost love as it is wondering how and when love will happen next or if love will ever happen again because in this vale of Vaseline and tears, whatever is given is also taken away. Love opens in the exact space of wondering what my chances are and figuring the hopeless odds against love. Then, biff, bam. Just when you least expect it, Monk says. Having known love before, I'm both a lucky one, ahead of the game, and also scared to death by memories of how sweet it is, how sad something that takes only a small bit of anybody's time can't be found more copiously, falling as spring rain or sunlight these simple things remind me of you and still do do do when Monk scatters notes like he's barefoot feeding chickenfeed to chickens or bleeding drop by drop precious Lord in the snow.

I believe when we're born each of us receives an invisible ladder we're meant to climb. We commence slowly, little baby shaky steps. Then bolder steps as we get the hang of it. Learn our powers, learn the curious construction of these ladders leaning on air, how the rungs are placed irregularly, almost as if they customize themselves to our stepping sometimes, so when we need them they're there or seem to be there solid under our feet because we're steady climbing and everybody around us steady climbing till it seems these invisible ladders, measure by measure, are music we perform as easily as breathing. Playing our song, we smile shyly, uneasily, the few times we remember how high and wide we've propelled ourselves into thin air step by step on rungs we never see disappearing behind us. And you can guess the rest of that tune, Monk says.

You place your foot as you always do, do, do, one in front of the other, then risk as you always do, do, do your weight on it so the other foot can catch up. Instead of dance music you hear a silent wind in your ears, blood pounding your temples, you're inside a house swept up in a tornado and it's about to pop, you're about to come tumbling down.

When your love starts to falling. Don't blame the missing rung. The ladder's still there. A bridge of sighs, of notes hanging in the air. A quicksilver run down the piano keys, each rib real as it's touched, then gone, wiped clean as Monk's hand flies glissando in the other direction.

One night in Paris trying to read myself to sleep, I heard the silence of rain. You might call silence a caesura, a break in a line of verse, the line pausing naturally to breathe, right on time, on a dime. But always a chance the line will never finish because the pause that refreshes can also swallow everything to the right and left of it.

Smoke curls from a gun barrel. The old poet, dissed by his young lover, shoots him, is on his way to jail. Rimbaud recovers from the wound, heads south toward long, long silence. Standing on a steamer's deck, baseball cap backward on his head, elbows on the rail, baggy pants drooping past the crack of his ass, Rimbaud sees the sea blistered by many dreamers like himself who leap off ships when no one's looking, as if the arc of their falling will never end, as if the fall can't be real because nobody sees it or hears it, as if they might return to their beginnings and receive another chance, as if the fall will heal them, a hot torch welding shut the black hole, the mouth from which silence issues thick as smoke from necklaces of burning tires.

Monk speaks many languages. The same sound may have different meanings in different languages. (To say = *tu sais* =

you know.) And the same sound may also produce different silences. To say nothing is not necessarily to know nothing. The same letters can represent different sounds. Or different letters equal the same sound (pane, pain, payne). In different languages or the same. A lovers' quarrel in the rain at the train station. The budding poet seals his lips evermore. The older man trims his words to sonnets, willed silence caging sound. Their quarrel echoes over and over again, what was said and not said and unsaid returns. The heart (ancient liar/lyre) hunched on its chair watching silent reruns, lip-synching new words to old songs.

Monk's through playing and everybody in the joint happy as a congregation of seals full of fish. He sits on the piano bench, hulking, mute, his legs chopped off at the knees like a Tutsi's by his fellow countrymen, listening in the dark to their hands coming together, making no sound. Sits till kingdom come, a giant sponge or ink blotter soaking up first all the light, then the air, then sucking all sound from the darkness, from the stage, the auditorium. The entire glittering city shuts down. Everything caves in, free at last in this bone-dry house.

Silence. Monk's. Mine. Yours. I haven't delved into mine very deeply yet, have I, avoid my silence like a plague, even though the disease I'm hiding from already rampant in my blood, bones, the air.

Where are you? How far to your apartment from the Woodside exit? What color are your eyes? Is your hair long or short? I know your father's gone. I met a taxi driver who happened to be from your home town, a friendly, talkative brother about your father's age, so I asked him if he knew your dad, figuring there would have been a colored part of your town and everybody would sort of know everybody else the way they used to in the places where people like our parents were raised. Yeah, oh yeah. Course I knew Henry Diggs, he said. Said he'd grown up knowing your dad and matter of fact had spoken with him in the American Legion Club not too long before he heard your father had died. Whatever took your father, it took him fast, the man said. Seemed fine at the club. Little thin maybe but Henry always been a neat, trim-looking fellow and the next thing I heard he was gone. Had that conversation with a cabdriver about five years ago and the way he talked about your dad I could picture him neat and trim and straight-backed, clear-eyed. Then I realized the picture out-of-date. Twenty years since I'd seen your father last and I hadn't thought much about him since. Picture wasn't actually a picture anyway. When I say picture I guess I mean the taxi driver's words made your father real again by shaking up the silence. Confirmed something about your dad. About me. The first time I met your father and shook his hand, I noticed your color, your cheekbones in his face. That's what I'd look for in his different face if someone pointed out an old man and whispered your father's name. You singing in his silent features.

Picturing you also seems to work till I try to really see the picture. Make it stand still, frame it. View it. Then it's not a picture. It's a wish. A yearning. Many images layered one atop the other, passing through one another, each one so fragile it begins to fade, to dance, give way to the next before I can fix you in my mind. No matter how gently I lift the veil, your face comes away with it . . .

James Brown the hardest worker in show biz, drops down on one knee. Please. Please. Please. Don't go. A spotlight fixes the singer on a darkened stage. You see every blister of sweat on his glistening skin, each teardrop like a bedbug crawling down the black satin pillowcase of his cheeks. Please. Please. Please. But nobody answers. Cause nobody's home. She took his love and gone. J.B. dies a little bit onstage. Then more and more. His spangled cape shimmers where he tossed it, a bright pool at the edge of the stage where someone he loves dived in and never came up.

Silence a good way of listening for news. Please. Please. Is anybody out there? The singer can't see beyond the smoking cone of light raining on his shoulders, light white from outside, midnight blue if you're inside it. Silence is Please. Silence is Please Please Please hollered till it hurts. Noise no one hears if no one's listening. And night after night evidently they ain't.

Who wants to hear the lost one's name? Who has the nerve to say it? Monk taps it out, depressing the keys, stitching messages his machine launches into the make-believe of hearts. Hyperspace. Monk folded over his console. Mothership. Mothership. Beam me up, motherfucker. It's cold down here.

Brother Sam Cooke squeezed into a phone booth and the girl can't help it when she catches him red-handed in the act of loving somebody else behind the glass. With a single shot she blows him away. But he's unforgettable, returns many nights. Don't cry. Don't cry. No, no, no — no. Don't cry.

My silence? Mine. My silence is, as you see, as you hear, sometimes broken by Monk's music, by the words of his stories. My silence not like Monk's, not waiting for what comes next to arrive or go on about its goddamned business. I'm missing someone. My story is about losing you. About not gripping tight enough for fear my fingers would close on air. Love, if we get it, as close to music as most of us get, and in Monk's piano solos I hear your comings and goings, tiptoeing in and out of rooms, in and out of my heart, hear you like I hear the silence there would be no music without, the silence saying the song could end at this moment, any moment silence plays around. Because it always does, if you listen closely. Before the next note plays, silence always there.

Three-thirty in the A.M. I'm wide awake and alone. Both glow-in-the-dark clocks say so — the square one across the room, the watch on the table beside the bed, they agree, except for a ten-minute discrepancy, like a longstanding quarrel in an old marriage. I don't take sides. Treat them both as if there is something out there in the silence yet to be resolved, as if the hands of these clocks are waiting as I am for a signal so they can align themselves perfectly with it.

I lie in my bed a thousand years. Aching silently for you. My arms crossed on my chest, heavy as stones, a burden awhile, then dust trickling through the cage of ribs, until the whole carcass collapses in on itself, soundlessly, a heap of fine powder finally the wind scatters, each particle a note unplayed, returned perfectly intact, back where it came from.

When Monk finishes work it's nearly dawn. He crosses Fifty-seventh Street, a cigarette he's forgotten to light dangling from his lower lip.

What-up, Monk.

Uh-huh.

Moon shines on both sides of the street. People pour from lobbies of tall hotels, carrying umbrellas. Confetti hang-glides, glittery as tinsel. A uniformed brass band marches into view, all the players spry, wrinkled old men, the familiar hymn they toot and tap and whistle and bang thrashes and ripples like a tiger caught by its tail.

Folks form a conga line, no, it's a second line hustling to catch up to Monk, who's just now noticed all the commotion behind him. The twelve white horses pulling his coffin are high steppers, stallions graceful, big-butted, and stylized as Rockettes. They stutter-step, freeze, raise one foreleg bent at the knee, shake it like shaking cayenne pepper on gumbo. The horses also have the corner boys' slack-leg, drag-leg pimp-strut down pat and perform it off-time in unison to the crowd's delighted squeals down Broadway while the brass band cooks and hordes of sparrow-quick pickaninnies and rump-roast-rumped church ladies wearing hats so big you think helicopter blades or two wings to hide their faces and players so spatted and chained, ringed and polished, you mize well concede everything you own to them before the game starts, everybody out marching and dancing behind Mr. Monk's bier, smoke from the cigarette he's mercifully lit to cut the funk drifting back over them, weightless as a blessing, as a fingertip grazing a note not played.

In my dream, we're kissing goodbye when Monk arrives. First his music, and then the great man himself. All the air rushes from my lungs. Thelonious Apoplecticus, immensely enlarged in girth, his cheeks puffed out like Dizzy's. He's sputtering and stuttering, exasperated, pissed off as can be. Squeaky chipmunk voice like a record playing at the wrong speed, the way they say Big O trash-talked on the b-ball court or deep-sea divers squeak if raised too rapidly from great depths. Peepy dolphin pip pip peeps, yet I understand exactly.

Are you crazy, boy. Telling my story. Putting mouth in my words. Speechless as my music rendered your simple ass on countless occasions, what kind of bullshit payback is this? Tutti-frutti motherfucker. Speaking for me. Putting your jive woogie in my boogie.

Say what, nigger? Who said I retreated to silence? Retreat hell. I was attacking in another direction.

The neat goatee and mustache he favored a raggedy wreath now, surrounding his entire moon face. He resembles certain Hindu gods with his nappy aura, his new dready cap of afterbirth in flames to his shoulders. Monk shuffles and grunts, dismisses me with a wave of his glowing hand. When it's time, when he feels like it, he'll play the note we've been waiting for. The note we thought was lost in silence. And won't it be worth the wait.

Won't it be a wonder. And meanwhile, love, while we listen, these foolish things remind me of you.

Are Dreams Faster Than
the Speed of Light

H E'D PLAYED those idle, whistling-in-the-dark games
with friends. If you had to choose, which would you
rather be, blind or deaf. Lose your arms or legs. With only
twenty-four hours to live, how would you spend your last day.
Well, someone not playing games had turned the games real.
The doctors couldn't tell him exactly how long he'd live but
could estimate plus or minus a couple months how long it
would be before he'd want to die. A long or short year from
today, they said, he'd enter final storms of outrageous suffering
and the disease he wouldn't wish on a dog that had just bitten
a hole in his ass, the disease he calls X cause its name's almost
as ugly as its symptoms, would shrink his muscles into Frito
corn curls and saw through one by one, millimeter by millimeter, with excruciating slowness all the cords stringing him along
with the illusion he's the puppet master of his limbs, and dry up
his lungs so they harden, burn, and crumble and he'll cough
them up in great heaving spasms of black-flecked phlegm. No
one knew the precise day or hour but sure as shit, given his
symptoms—the jiggle in his legs, spiraling auras wiggling
through the left side of his field of vision, numbness of tongue,
fasciculations everywhere rippling like a million snakes under
his skin, bone-aching weariness totally out of proportion to the
minimal bit of physical activity required to survive day by day—
the specialists agreed unanimously his ass was grass, maybe

he'd last one more Christmas, if lucky, just in time to beg Santa for death if death hadn't already come creeping and smirking into his room.

The riot of pain the doctors promised doesn't scare him. Drugs will dull most of it, won't they. He just hates the anticipation. Always prided himself on being the kind of guy who liked to bull-rush the enemy, get it on, get it over. As long as he had a chance to fight back, he could handle whatever. From day one, his color plus a jock mentality had turned every encounter into a contest. Even the smallest choices. For the past year he'd believed the tremor in his hands a symptom of his crazy habit of always needing to win. You reach for the pepper and at the last instant, because your mind's still debating the pluses and minuses of whether to sprinkle pepper or salt on your pasta, your hand hesitates, flutters in the air above the nearly identical shakers. Sometimes you knock over stuff. Sometimes you laugh at yourself. Sometimes you want to scream. To kill. Or die. Each decision a drama. Your fate and the future of Western civilization hinge on whether you top your coffee with a dab of half-and-half or a dollop of skim milk.

Now it turns out the problem not indecision, not fear of doing the wrong thing and losing. No. Not his wacky mind causing his hands to tremble. His body's wacky. Loose connections in the circuitry of nerves. Connections blocked by inflamed tissue and arthritic bones. Simple motions frustrated by lack of information. Muscles atrophying because they don't receive enough love from the brain. They forget how to contract or stretch. All the switchboard operators sprawled dead or dying after a terrorist raid.

When his eyes slink open in the morning he tells himself, You're still here, nothing's different. Nothing to worry about, anyway. Over is over. Once gone, you're really gone. It's the air conditioner, the fridge, stupid, not death droning in your ear. Crowds amaze him. Busy swarms of people who haven't heard the news. Hey, he wants to shout. Listen up, everybody. It ain't just about me. Each and every one of you has got to go. For sure. Damned sure. Maybe the woman scowling into her paperback or that guy propped half asleep against the pole will be gone before this year's up. How would the others packed at this particular moment into this particular subway car behave if they knew what he knew. Knew their score. A week, ten days, a long or short year. Would their hearts beat faster when they tried to figure out what to do next, tried to figure out what this time means, this minute or day or month remaining. Everything and nothing. Would they hear each click of a faceless clock counting down what's left of their lives. Would they understand they'd never understand. Not even this simplest thing about being on the earth. Caught in a net that's nothing but holes.

The doctors say his time's almost up and suddenly he's old, just about as old as he'll ever get. An old man, all the people who once mattered long gone so the death sentence a fresh start too. He owes nothing to anyone. Owns the little time left. Though he can't afford to waste a second, no rush either. Size doesn't matter. Everybody gets a whole life — beginning, middle, end — no matter how quickly it's over. Like those insects *ephemerids* he'd read about, their entire life cycle squeezed into an hour of a May afternoon. Like his siblings, the twin boy and girl who couldn't stick around long enough to receive names, dying a few hours after birth, taking his sweet, sweet mother with them.

How long does it take to die. Well . . . that, of course, depends on many factors . . . He watches the doctor's face, watches himself lean forward, and in a weird way he's watcher and watched, patient and doctor, weather and weatherman. The doc's gleaming brow reassures, sleek flesh befitting his whopping fees, the location of his office, the trust you must invest in his words, healthy sheen, vacation tan. Tiny ellipsoid spectacles slide down his nose a smidgen as he closes a smidgen the distance between you, kisser and kissed. He's seen the same commercials you have, represents just this side of convincingly the actor acting like a doctor, this doc with big hands and big face and a habit of staring offstage at the imponderably heavy-duty shit always lurking just beyond the high-definition scene in which the two of you are engaged in delicate conversation about fate—your fate, not his, because this doctor's a permanent member of the cast, always available to move the plot along, advise, console, subtle as a brick revealing the brutal verdict. I've never figured out how to inform the patient, he confides. Fortunately, I don't see cases like yours very often. What can I say, except it's one of those things in life we must adjust to as best we can. Nobody ever said it was going to be easy. It's a job and somebody has to do it, somebody's got to die. Did the doc really say that. Was he complaining about his tough job or commiserating with his patient. Does it matter. He steals the doctor's voice again, pipes it through the plane. This is your captain speaking . . . We are experiencing an emergency. Please remove the oxygen mask of the helpless passenger beside you before you remove yours.

He'd begun compiling a list of chores, necessary things to do to prepare for the end. A notebook page full before he realized the list was about expecting time, using time, filling time, about plans, control, the future, wishful thinking, as if time were at his disposal. As if he possessed the power to choose—blind or deaf—as those silly scare games proposed. As if he weren't already eyeless, crippled, helpless, just about out of time. Next move always the last move. When he switched the list to *must do,* he was relieved by its shortness. Only two items: he must die, and before his time's up he must end the bad ending of his father's life. Couldn't leave his poor daddy behind to suffer any longer—how long, how long. He must take his father's life.

An unimaginable thought at first. How in hell could you kill murder whack terminate snuff your own father. Ashamed of the thought, then guilty when he doesn't act. If he loves his father, why allow him to suffer. Somebody needs to step up to the plate. Who, if not him. In the limbo of the veterans' hospital his father's shrinking body, in spite of its skinny frailty, of the burden of its diseased mind, might not fail for years. Meaningless years in terms of quality of life his father could expect, meaningless except for whatever it means when a fatally wounded animal suffers, means when an intensely proud, private man whose major accomplishment in life was maintaining a fierce independence winds up on display, naked, paddling around in his own shit. Cruel years of pointless hanging on. Years the son does not have now, thus different now, on his mind daily, monopolizing the little time, his only time remaining.

The father so present dying, so absent alive. For years, decades, starting even before his daddy had passed him to his grandmothers and aunts to raise, they'd been losing touch, becoming two men who see each other infrequently, not exactly strangers, more like longstanding acquaintances who hook up now and then in restaurants or bars, talk ball games, politics, an easy, no-strings-attached fondness. They observe an almost courtly politeness and restraint, as if questions about the other's personal life would be not only prying but breaking the rules, a kind of betrayal even, an admission of desiring more than the other so far had given and thus a rebuke, whiny dissatisfaction, after all these years, with an arrangement formed by mutual consent that had seemed to serve them both well enough.

Since he wasn't God and couldn't simply will his father's death and be done with it, killing his father necessitated tending to messy details. A weapon, for instance. And words, his unreliable weapon of choice, wouldn't suffice in this crisis, either. Wouldn't buy more time. Or finish his father's time. Yet a word, *hemlock,* popped into his mind, clarified options. A quick, lethal does of poison no doubt the most efficient, practical means of accomplishing the dirty work. Hemlock shorthand for his plan, code word for whatever poison he might procure. Hemlock certainly sounded nicer than strychnine, anthrax, arsenic, cyanide, cyclone B — poisons he associated with murder mysteries, pest exterminators, concentration camps. After repeating the word to himself many times, it took on a life of its own: Hemlock, a cute, sleepy-eyed little turtle. Hemlock finally because it reminded him of the painting.

During its first year, when the veterans' hospital was overstaffed and underused, only a small group of patients occupied the locked-down seventh-floor ward, and walking the brand-new halls with his father, he'd been reassured without realizing it by an illusion of spaciousness and tranquillity some clever architect had contrived with high ceilings, tall windows, gleaming floor tiles, unadorned planes of wall like a gallery stripped for the next exhibition. Almost as if he strolled with his father through that familiar classic painting, the one whose title he couldn't recall then or now, *The Academy of So-and-so at Somewhere,* he thinks, remembering a slide from a college survey of art, philosophers in togas, their elegant postures, serious demeanors, a marble dome, sky-roofed arcades, a scene, said the voiceover, embodying intricate thought, calm speculation, the slow, careful accumulation of beads of truth on invisible threads connecting Socrates to Plato, Plato to Aristotle, Aristotle to Virgil or Dante or the pope, whoever these bearded, antique figures populating the painting were supposed to depict, wherever the idyllic version of Greece or Rome was supposed to exist, living and dead in earnest conversation — maybe it's heaven, the strollers immortals, maybe he had needed to flee that far away from the nearly empty, spic-and-span scrubbed corridors of the seventh-floor ward to feel what he felt then and wishes he could feel again: the peace, false or not, of those first walks now that everything has changed, very aware now, mainly because it's missing and irretrievable, of the comforting illusion he'd once enjoyed, the sense of order and safety impossible today beside his father in a traffic jam of shambling, drugged, dull-eyed, muttering men in aqua pajamas, father and son slowly shuffling back and forth along corridors where windows begin above their shoulders and ascend to the top of high off-white walls, giant glass panels cloning light but allowing no one to see in, no one to see out.

Did the building in the painting have a basement, under-ground kennels the artist chose not to include. Where were the people who clean and polish the marble. Where were the sick and dying. The maimed in body and spirit. Where were the good citizens with brown faces who look like us, Daddy, who are doomed like us, Daddy.

Are dreams faster than the speed of light. Should he ask his father. Wouldn't his daddy know all the answers now, the whole truth and nothing but the truth tucked away in his silence, si-lence deep as the painting's, his father mute like those white-robed sages frozen beneath a canopy of marble arches, all the time in the world on their hands, the ever blue Mediterranean sky at bay above their heads.

He stands pressed into a tall corner watching his father, a brown, wooden man on the barber's wooden stool. Next to his father on a folding chair another aqua-pajamaed man, face pale as the ghostly philosophers', a dentist they say in his other life, babbles nonstop, cracking himself up, ha-ha-ha-ha as if he's still the life of the party, entertaining a captive audience of dental technicians and patients in the tooth-pulling parlor where he reigns until it's his turn on the stool.

The barber, who comes on Tuesdays and Thursdays to the VA hospital and sets up shop in an alcove near the nurses' sta-tion so he can holler for help if a patient gets unruly, snips, snips, snips, scissors snipping like a patient swarm of insects darting around his father's head. A crown of snips if you drew lines from one snip to the next. The black-handled scissors restore the handsome, well-groomed man his father has always been, disguise the madness lying in wait to seize his features. Scissors snip, snip, snipping, the barber intent as Babo in Melville's *Benito Cereno,* as Michelangelo coaxing the sleeping David from a block of marble, like the voice trimming and snipping these words, these words words words snipping, killing, drifting away, white hairs, brown hairs, gray hairs, little commas and tightly curled spirals that accumulate on the cloth draping his father's shoulders, hairs that have grown too long and wild, telling tales *Beware, beware, his flashing eyes and floating hair* on the tight-lipped, vacant-eyed man shuffling toward you in one of the corridors radiating like spokes from the panopticon hub of the nurses' station.

His father's face looking good, holding on in spite of scalding daylight powering from the window above the alcove. Still a striking face, a brown-eyed, handsome man, uh-huh, *he was a brown-eyed handsome man,* this pretty daddy who stares without blinking at a landscape only he's able to see, a place elsewhere demanding more and more of his attention until one day his father had shrugged his shoulders and let the weight of this world slip off his back. As simple as that. As simple and quick as standing up when the barber finishes and letting the white cloth drop behind you onto the empty stool.

Are dreams faster than the speed of light. He had asked himself the question after Lisa related a story about a Chinese physicist at Cal Tech or Berkeley or UCLA, he doesn't remember which university, just the fact it was a West Coast school because he recalls imagining out loud a life for the scientist, how the guy winds up in charge of a world-class experimental physics lab after being born in an internment camp out West. Would a spotless lab coat, a droptop BMW erase memories of almost starving to death, a nisei father killed defending American interests in the Pacific, the bittersweet day of release from the camp, his mother's tears, her brown hands eternally cracked from trying to grow food in Arizona sand, wait a minute Lisa interrupts in the middle of my riff, *Chinese* not Japanese, she says, but who cares about such fine distinctions when war fever's high, he says. A chink's a chink. Yellow peril. Yellow menace. This article's about today, not World War Two, stupid, so stop raving, she says, waving in his face a clipping from the *Times* that describes an experiment a Chinese scientist conducted and experts from around the world either hailed enthusiastically or dissed as a crock of inscrutable shit, the division of opinion duly noted and quoted so discriminating readers of the science section could decide for themselves.

Something about light waves behaving weirdly when superheated in a bath of cesium. Light wave/particles accelerated till they're simultaneously here and there, present and absent, moving faster than light's supposed to move, faster than 186,000 miles per second, the speed everybody agreed till now nothing can move faster than. About kung fu a Chinese physicist performed with microwaves, mirrors, and lasers, a trick comparable to marking and releasing a rat before it's been captured. The scientist proving with measurements of before and after that no reliable measurements of before and after exist, since the rat/light breaks free on the far side of the labyrinth at precisely the instant it's about to enter. One impossibility — motion faster than the speed of light — proving another impossibility possible. You know, like a unicorn's mother appearing on *Oprah* with a photo of the son she's begging viewers to help her locate.

Wow. Flying faster than the speed of light you could travel through time, Lisa hollers. And then, as if the news too urgent to wait till she finishes showering, she shouts through the bathroom door, A person could be in two places at once.

I'm always in two places, he almost shouts back. Too goddamned many different places at once, thinking of himself dispersed as data on some marketing consultant's spreadsheet or as a blip on a Pentagon doomsday planner's screen estimating acceptable first-strike losses. His mom in heaven, smiling down on him. Hungry worms slithering in the mud smiling up. Here. There. Everywhere. In a different place from Lisa, as usual. Locked up in one of America's concentration camps while she hitchhikes through history.

Do you think this advance in science will prevent roundups of civilians, rape, torture, mass exterminations in the next world war, my sweet.

C'mon. Stop being a grouch, Lisa says. And he decides to let her enthusiasm infect him, especially since she's standing beside the bed naked. Why worry about his looming death. Why not thank goodness no world war at present. None he's aware of, at least. Lots of small flare-ups, police actions, rebels in the hills, terrorists, spasms of ethnic cleansing, etc., but no knock-down-drag-out global conflict, unless Big War too has learned to be in many places at once, no place and everywhere, like the rat, the particles. Like him.

He intended to keep the clipping, can't remember if he did or where he might have stashed it, but recalls they'd made love not war that night. Lisa moist and warm from her shower, his hand running up and down her thigh, fingertips tickling her hipbone, the smooth hollow of her flank, his hand sliding around and up to sample the flat, limber strength above her butt's *mmmmm good,* buttery curve.

Your father's a fine-looking man, sir, the barber says, stepping back from the stool to admire his handiwork. Does he expect a tip. Where's the motormouth dentist who was next.

No sign his father heard the barber. No sign his father still on the planet except for the shell of body abandoned on the stool.

Hey. Yo. You. Mr. brown-eyed, handsome Bojangles man, the barber turned you into a movie star, mister. All the ladies swoon, they see you struttin' down the avenue.

Does the man on the stool respond with the slightest of twinkles, a tiny, teasy pursing upturn of one corner of his mouth, Daddy's way, his way. Do the man's eyeballs roll toward the ceiling because his son's talking trash, or is he remembering scissors, remembering he must sit very still to avoid danger in the air above his head, the helicopter blades still up there snip-snipping, clipping away hair, bone, brain if you're not careful. If you make a sudden wrong move.

Later, walking the ward, fingers pinching his father's blue-green sleeve, he thinks you could call it a freak show — that one's glare, this one's wailing, that poor soul sitting on the side of the bed diddling himself, pajama bottoms down around his ankles — or just concede craziness its due, let craziness convince, let it suck you in or the effort of resisting can make you crazy. When it comes to reality, one man, one vote. Purest democracy on the seventh floor. Equal opportunity votes for men who believe they're women. Only the doctors and staff try to convert. But no sudden turnabouts here. No compromises, deals, consensus. Each aqua fish swims in a different sea. Even when they bump or fight or scream at each other, the water's different for each one. Different bumps, different fights. Real craziness is believing otherwise.

On the seventh floor the sensible question always *why not*. Why isn't his father's tale of a nurse fondling him a possibility. Not a tale exactly. His father couldn't string enough words together to construct a tale. A kind of sweet wonderment, a be-dazzled grogginess in his father's voice and movements, pleasure expressed with body language, winks, sighs, exclamations, his large, knotty hands eloquently molding shapes out of thin air. Signs of a very intimate encounter a slightly embarrassed son must witness. Maybe an incident earlier this morning. Or days before or weeks or never. For sure it's happening now. A minidrama staged on the screen of his daddy's face. Is his father frowning because he's suddenly been deserted by his angel, required to speak to the figure beside him, a figure bewildering till it morphs again into a woman with soft, curious hands, her warmth, her perfume melting him, lifting him, then the beam of her dissolves to his son and he wants the son to meet this nice lady, the pretty woman he can't say with words, who breaks apart and floats away when he reaches for her, for the next word, for a way to keep her or let her go while he explains her to this ghost who claims to be his son.

As if I know. *As if I'll ever know. As if anybody ever knows.* Hard enough to live in his own dreams. A nightmare of emaciated naked people passing by in an endless line. His job hosing them down before they vanish in roiling clouds of disinfectant that's also poisonous gas. Then he's knee-deep in piles of bloody, contorted corpses he must untangle, arrange in neat rows according to gender color age size. A nightmare equal parts Holocaust and Middle Passage and him equal parts victim and executioner. The whole evil concoction like a program he's watching on the History Channel, safe until it snatches him inside and the images on the screen are his memories, his heart pounding because he knows his father's lollipop head will scroll by on one of those stick people, his father's face, his own, face after familiar face asking why, why, why are we here and you there, why are you combing through heaps of mangled dead bodies searching for us when we're beside you, right here in front of your eyes.

Maybe a routine wash-up his father is embellishing. An aide's daily chore to change the soiled diaper, scrub the old man clean, shave him, perhaps oil and talc his skin. A particularly kind nurse reminded of a father or husband or son or lover by this good-looking, helpless, brown-skinned man, gentle, gentle as a newborn on his good days. An extra portion of TLC administered. Her soft, firm hands massage bare shoulders and back. His father amazed. Reminded of the truth of himself. Of desire belonging to him, the terrifying, demanding return of focus when the fog is pierced and a bright, solid world of haunt-ing clarity streams through the needle's eye *faster than the speed of light.*

Tell me again, son. I hate to keep asking you to repeat things but it's getting harder and harder for your old father to keep it all straight. Play my numbers in the tobacco shop over by where Sears used to be, you know, over there on Hiland Av-enue. Walk out the tobacco shop and half-hour later can't re-member whether I played my goddamn figures or not. It's vex-ing, vexing. Standing there on the sidewalk not knowing what I did or didn't do. Come next morning I think about putting my numbers in and damn, realize I ain't checked what hit yes-terday. Forget to check, forget if I played or not, forget there's a goddamn lottery, forget all that money white people owe me. What I'm trying to say is I know you already told me once, but I can't keep nothing straight in this feeble-ass mind of mine any-more. So tell me again, son. Why do I have to die. Why you have to kill me.

The academy's retractable roof opens and warm starlight bathes father and son. Lutes strum just loud enough to be heard, not exactly breaking the silence, more a reminder of si-lence, a pulse within night's quiet, this night with qualities of day exhaling the freshly scrubbed breath of dawn. His father's face glows. A zigzag vein pulses in his temple. His proud, high forehead imposing as the brows of Benin nobles sculpted in bronze.

Levitating like Yoruba priests he'd read about, they float two or three inches above the treadmill looping of a path contrived to convince you you're strolling or running or flying faster than the speed of light and the sham works until a moment like this one beside his father, when he peers down and observes the pe-culiar laxness of their ankles, their dangling feet not quite brushing the path that revolves beneath them, feet supple as fins, as the naked, boneless feet of blond angels hovering and strumming lutes in the ether of medieval illuminations. Not very high but sufficiently high to understand they are being taken for a ride, each step forward on the rotating path also a step in place, a step backward, the world surrounding them a painted backdrop or dancing shadows on a screen, you know, the way a filmstrip projected behind stationary actors animates Hollywood scenes, just mirrors and shuck and jive, the son understands, gazing down past his father's mashed-back slippers, his own clownish, overbuilt, winged sneakers, shoes tied to feet tied to ankles limp as a lynched man, shoes freed of the body's weight, trussed-up feet going nowhere fast, a mountain of empty shoes, shoes, shoes, late and soon.

It's about me, Daddy. Not you. Something awful's happening to me. The doctors say I have just a little time left. And some of it will be bad, very bad. The disease killing me will kick up its heels and party hearty. Oh-la-la, Daddy. I'm not scared for myself, but I'm scared for you. Don't want to leave you behind to suffer.

His father's head droops. Perfect haircut, courtesy of the state, intact. He could be nodding or he could be ratcheting down one notch further into Zombieville.

Why his father and no one else. Why did he confess the dirty secret of the disease only to his father. If Lisa was as helpless as his father, would he have shared the news of his death with her. The huge, trifling news. All these years assiduously looking out for himself as if he'd been entrusted with a project of cosmic significance. Hmmmm. Not much to him after all. Maybe that's why he hoarded his news. No news, really. No big thing. Everyone dies sooner or later and oop-poop-a-doop, surprise—surprise—one less monkey don't stop no show. Did he believe withholding his little secret would inflate it into big news. Wasn't he like those homeless particle waves flying faster than the speed of light—gone, gone before he even got here.

Only once, when she was leaning over the sink, intent on

cleaning up a mess they'd made, her thin back looking even smaller with her little girl's shoulders hunched forward, both arms invisible from where he sat, only that once had he almost said to anyone other than his father, I'm going to be very sick and soon after that I'll die. Dressed for court in elegant business suits with short skirts and double-breasted jackets, shiny panty-hose encasing shapely legs, black hair precisely bobbed, Lisa could transform herself into a cartel-busting, justice-for-the-wretched-of-the-earth, petite Abrams tank. He'd feel proud of her glamour, her gleaming impenetrability and incorruptibility. When she smiled at him, testing him one last time on the intricate maneuvers required to mesh and unmesh his sloth with her complicated schedule that particular day, he loved her, loved how full of herself, how undaunted she could be, marveled at the distance between them, distance they sometimes miraculously closed, but distance that also stunned him each morning. Would he matter enough to woo her back. Slouched in the fat chair, staring at the stalled novel in his notebook, he'd exhale a sigh of relief after the door closed behind her slim, perfect hips, hopelessly missing her, but also glad she was gone so he could get on with the rest of his life.

After the phone rings, in the instant between recognizing Lil Sis's voice and listening to what Lil Sis is saying, he wonders why he hadn't thought of her, isn't Lil Sis the perfect person to tell the news of his death, this stranger, this half-sister, strangely closer now because the father they share, a stranger during his life to both of them, is dying. Should he tell her about hemlock too.

Hate to call with bad news, but Daddy's had a fall. Doesn't sound too good. The doctor wants to operate right away.

A fall.

That's what they claim. But you know as well as I do the rough stuff goes on at the VA. They say one of the nurses found him lying on the floor and Daddy couldn't get up. Sounds like his hip busted up really badly. In splinters, they say. Lots of bleeding inside the joint and that's why they have to operate quick, before it gets infected. I want to know how in hell he wound up on the floor. But Daddy can't tell us, so I guess we'll never find out, will we.

Operate how soon.

If we say okay, they'll try to schedule him for tomorrow morning.

After he hangs up the phone, he thinks he should have said no. Let nature take its goddamn course. Out of it as his father already is, he'll be worse after surgery. Old people can't deal with anesthesia. His grandfather never the same after they knocked him out and cut on him.

But you can't just let a person rot. Surgery or not, his own rot-smart bones whisper, this mugging will finish off your father. Is he just a tiny bit disappointed he's lost the chance to play hero. After all the agonizing, rationalizing, and fighting with himself, finally, a rush of cool determination. Clarity at last. Yes, yes. Ready to purchase poison, activate the plan. A hemlocked vanilla milkshake the final solution. A special treat he'd bring to the hospital next Sunday. Vanilla milkshake my dad's favorite thing, folks. Sharing one with him for old time's sake. Father and son on the last train out of Dodge. A carefully drafted note in plain view on the bedside table explaining everything so nobody gets the wrong idea.

To top off the plan, he'd prepay a double funeral. Ride off with his daddy in a horse-drawn black hearse. A glorious New Orleans goodbye parade winding through the streets of Homewood. The Pittsburgh Rockets Drum and Bugle Corps leading the march. Shiny trumpets and tubas. Umpah-umpah. Ratta-tat-tat-tat. Tease of jive and boogie in their mournful playing, their precise highstepping. Barbequed kielbasa with red-hot sauce. Coolers full of icy Iron City. Hmmm. Oh, didn't we ramble, Daddy. Oh, didn't we.

You never know, do you.

The big-eared, retro phone smirks at him. So much ado about nothing. No opportunity, after all, to play God. Game called on account of rain. The coy old AME Zion deity working in his own good time his wonders to perform.

At the hospital, not counting his father, three of them in the room when a nurse breezes in to brief the family. Very sound reasons not to count his father, but how could you ever be sure. Introducing himself as Clarence, folks, the nurse flashes a silver-starred front tooth. In six months, if he lives that long, will his eyes still be able to read the tattoo on the nurse's hairy forearm. A posse of needles, tubes, gauges, pumps, suction, drips protects the bed. Virtual life puttering on forever in printouts, on screens, in beeping monitors, whether or not a glimmer of vitality in his father's eyes.

Of course, even now, at his dad's direst moment, at this sad, affecting denouement, the son flies elsewhere, faster than the speed of light, father forgotten, son dreaming ahead to what it will be like at his own miserable countdown. Shit, he's thinking. Shit. What's the point. What's the horseshit stinking point.

The nurse updates them.

We can't get Mr. Wideman to eat. Goes on to explain why it's important for patients to eat. Explains that patients die if we don't manage to start them eating post-op. Explains the options, mouthwise or IVs, folks, and how the mouthwise method is much preferred by doctors, staff, studies, you know. And next thing I know, after Lil Sis's husband and I crank up the bed, I'm standing beside my father waving a spoonful of vanilla ice cream (go figure) I'm supposed to coax, wheedle, beg, sneak, lever, ram down his throat. I try to steady my shaky hand. Inch the spoon closer, closer to cracked lips the exact shape and color of mine, lips I swam through like a fish when I was birthed a second time *John Edgar, John* my dead mother's dead father's name, *Edgar* my father's, both names chosen by my mother to bind me to the men she'd loved most in the world. *Entitles*, my South Carolina grandfather would have called the names my father whispered to Reverend Felder and the good reverend's bass intoned loudly to family and friends gathered around the baptismal font of Homewood AME Zion.

And dead as he is, as I am for all intents and purposes, I find myself touching my father's mouth, prying open a space between what dwells outside him and all that's indwelling, and then into the passage propped open by thumb and finger I attempt to slip a spoon, ease a spoon, pray a spoon the way I'd heard my mother on her knees pray, the entire congregation of Homewood AME Zion pray and chant Sunday mornings to a God I never could love, not even then, long ago when I was a boy, only fear, only address when I desired something very badly I knew I wasn't going to get anyway so why not ask, why not believe a different life possible, joining the other lives I daydreamed daily. Lives not in my father's house nor my mother's bosom nor God's bosom nor the streets of Homewood. Made-up lives like this one I try to save holding open my father's mouth.

His teeth chatter, his jaw twitches as uneven surges of air enter and leave. Losing most of the load maneuvering the spoon through a broken fence of snags anchored in corpse-foul gums, I keep Lil Sis busy wiping vanilla drool from our daddy's chin as I ladle what I can into him, down him, and nothing, nothing else matters.

Who Invented the Jump Shot

The native American rubber-ball game played on a masonry court has intrigued scholars of ancient history since the Spaniards redefined the societal underpinnings of the New World.

—Scarborough and Wilcox,
The Mesoamerican Ballgame

THE SEMINAR ROOM was packed. *Packed* as in crowded, *packed* as in a packed Supreme Court, *packed* as in a fresh-meat inmate getting his shit packed by booty bandits. In other words, the matter being investigated, "Who Invented the Jump Shot," (a) has drawn an overflow crowd of academics, (b) the fix is in, (c) I'm about to be cornholed without giving permission.

The title of the session let the cat out the bag. It advertised two false assumptions — that at some particular moment in time the jump shot had appeared, new and fully formed as Athena popping from the thigh of Zeus, and that a single individual deserved credit as inventor. "Who Invented the Jump Shot" will be a pissing contest. And guess who will win. Not my perpetually outnumbered, outvoted, outgunned side. Huh-uh. No way. My noncolored colleagues will claim one of their own, a white college kid on such and such a night, in such and such an obscure arena, proved by such and such musty, dusty documents, launched the first jump shot. Then they'll turn the session into a coming-out party for the scholar who invents the inventor. Same ole, same ole aggression, arrogance, and conspicuous consumption. By the end of the seminar's two hours they'll own the jump shot, unimpeachable experts on its birth, development, and death. Rewriting history, planting their flag on a chunk of territory because no native's around to holler, Stop, thief.

And here I sit, a colored co-conspirator in my lime-colored plastic contour chair, my transportation, food, and lodging complimentary, waiting for an answer to a question nobody with good sense would ask in the first place. Even though I've fired up more jumpers than all the members of the Association for the Study of Popular Culture combined, do you think anybody on the planning committee bothered to solicit my opinion on the shot's origins. With their linear, lock-step sense of time, their solipsism and bonehead priorities, no wonder these suckers can't dance.

Let's quietly exit from this crowded hall in a mega–conference center in Minneapolis and seek the origins of the jump shot elsewhere, in the darkness where my lost tribe wanders still.

Imagine the cramped interior of an automobile, a make and model extant in 1927, since that's the year we're touching down, on a snowy night inside, let's say, a Studebaker sedan humping down a highway, a car packed with the bodies of five large Negroes and a smallish driver whose pale, hairy-knuckled fingers grip the steering wheel. It's January 27, 1927, to be exact, and we're on our way from Chicago to Hinckley, Illinois, population 3,600, a town white as Ivory Snow, to play a basketball game against Hinckley's best for money.

Though he's not an athlete, the driver wears a basketball uniform under his shirt, you know, the way some men who are not women sport a bra and panties under their clothes, just in case. In any case, even if pressed into playing because the referee fouls out one of us, the driver's all business, not a player. A wannabe big-time wheeler-dealer but so far no big deal. Now he's got a better idea. He's noticed how much money white people will pay to see Negroes do what white people can't or won't or shouldn't but always wanted to do, especially after they see Negroes doing it. Big money in the pot at the end of that rainbow. Those old-time minstrel shows and medicine shows a goldmine and now black-faced hoofers and crooners starring in clubs downtown. Why not ball games. Step right up, ladies and gents. Watch Jimbo Crow fly. Up, up, and away with the greatest of ease. Barnstorming masters of thin air and striptease, of flim and flam and biff-bam-thank-you-mammy jamming.

Not the world-renowned Globies quite yet, and the jump shot not the killer weapon it will be one day, but we're on our way. Gotta start somewhere, so Mr. Abe the driver has rounded up a motley squad and the Globies' first tour has commenced humbly, if not exactly in obscurity, since we headed for Hinckley in daylight, or rather the dregs of daylight you get on overcast afternoons in gray, lakeside Chicago, 3:30 P.M. the time on somebody's watch when Pascal Rucker, the last pickup, grunts and fusses and stuffs his pivot man's bulk into the Studebaker's back seat and we're off.

Soon a flying highway bug *splat* invents the windshield. The driver's happy. Open road far as the eye can see. He whistles chorus after identical chorus, optimistically mangling a riff from a herky-jerky Satchmo jump. The driver believes in daylight. Believes in signing on the bottom line. Believes in the two-lane, rod-straight road, his sturdy automobile. He believes he'll put miles between Chicago and us before dark. Deliver his cargo to Hinckley on schedule. Mercifully, the whistling stops when giant white flakes begin to pummel us soundlessly. Shit, he mutters, shit, shit, then snorts, then announces, No sweat, boys. I'll get us to Hinckley. No sweat. Tarzan Smith twists round from the front seat, rolls his lemur eyes at me, *Right,* and I roll my eyes back at him, *Right.*

The Studebaker's hot engine strains through a colder than cold night. Occasional arrhythmic flutter-*fluups* interrupt the motor's drone, like the barely detectable but fatal heart murmurs of certain athletes, usually long, lean Americans of African descent who will suddenly expire young, seemingly healthy in the prime of their careers, a half-century later. *Fluups* worrying the driver, who knows the car's seriously overloaded. Should he pull over and let it rest. Hell, no, lunkhead. Just let it idle a while on the shoulder. Cut off the goddamn motor and who knows if it'll start up again. The driver imagines the carful of them marooned, popsicles stuck together till spring thaws this wilderness between Chicago and Hinckley. Slows to a creepy crawl. Can't run, can't hide. An easy target for the storm. It pounces, cuffs them from side to side of the highway, pisses great, sweeping sheets of snow spattering against the tin roof. How will he hear the next *fluup*. His head aches from listening. Each mile becomes minutes and minutes hours and hours stretch into an interminable wait between one *fluup* and the next. Did he hear the last one or imagine it. If *fluup*'s the sound of doom, does he really want to hear it again.

Some ungenerous people might suggest the anxious person hunched over the steering wheel obsesses on *fluups* to distract himself from the claustrophobia and scotophobia he can't help experiencing when he's the only white man stuck somewhere in the middle of nowhere with these colored guys he gets along with very well most of the time. C'mon. Give the driver a break. He rides, eats, drinks with them. To save money he'll sleep in the same room, the same bed, for Chrissakes, with one of them tonight. He'll be run out of godforsaken little midwestern towns with the players after they thump the locals too soundly. Nearly lynched when Foster grins back at a white woman's lingering Chessy-cat grin. Why question the driver's motives. Give the man the benefit of the doubt. Who are you, anyway, to cast the first brick.

Who handed you a striped shirt and whistle. In the driver's shoes — one cramping his toes, the other gingerly tapping the accelerator—you'd listen too. Everybody crazy enough to be out on the road tonight driving way too fast. As if pedal to the metal they can outrun weather, outrun accidents. You listen because you want to stay alive.

Or try to listen, try to stay alert in the drowsy heat of the car's interior, your interior hot and steamy too, anticipating a rear-end assault from some bootlegger's rattling, snub-nosed truck. Does he dare stomp harder on the gas. Can't see shit. The windshield ice-coated except for a semiclear, half-moon patch more or less the size of his soon-to-be roommate Smith's long bare foot. The driver leans forward, close enough to kiss the glass. Like looking at the world through the slot of one of those deep-sea diving helmets. Squinting to thread the car through the storm's needle eye makes his headache worse. Do his players believe he can see where he's going. Do they care. Two guys in the front seat trade choruses of snores. Is anybody paying attention. Blind as he is peering through snow-gritty glass, he might as well relax, swivel around, strike up a conversation if somebody's awake in the back.

It's fair to ask why, first thing, I'm inside the driver's head. Didn't we start out by fleeing a conference hall packed with heads like his. A carful of bloods and look whose brains I pick to pick. Is my own gray matter hopelessly whitewashed. Isn't the whole point of writing to escape what people not me think of me. In my defense I'll say it's too easy to feel what the players feel. Been there, done that. Too easy, too predictable. Of course not all players alike. Each one different from the other as each is different from the driver. But crammed in the Studebaker with someone not one of them at the wheel, players share a kind of culture, cause when you get right down to it, the shit's out of your hands, anybody's hands, ain't nowhere to go but where you're going so kick back and enjoy the ride. Or ignore the ride. Hibernate in your body, your good, strong, hungry player's body. Eat yourself during the long ride. Nourish your muscle with muscle, fat with fat, cannibalizing yourself to survive. Cause when the cargo door bangs open you better be ready to explode out the door. Save yourself. Hunker down. Body a chain and comfort. Body can be hurt, broken, disappear as smoke up a chimney, but because we're in this together, there's a temporary sense of belonging, of solidarity and weight while we anticipate the action we know is coming. Huge white flakes tumbling down outside, but you crouch warm inside your body's den, inside this cave of others like you who dream of winning or losing, of being a star or a chump, inventing futures that drift through your mind, changing your weatherscape, tossing and turning you in the busy land of an exile's sleep. If it ain't one thing it's another, raging outside the window, my brothers. Let it snow, let it snow, let it snow.

Whatever I pretend to be, I'm also one of them. One of us riding in our ancient, portable villages. Who's afraid of insane traffic, of howling plains, howling savages. *Howling. Savages.* Whoa. Where did those words come from. Who invented them. Treacherously, the enemy's narrative insinuates itself. Takes over before you realize what's going on. Howling savages. It's easy to stray. Backslide. Recycle incriminating words as if you believe the charges they contain. Found again. Lost again. *Howling savages.* Once you learn a language, do you speak it or does it speak you. Who comes out of your mouth when you use another's tongue. As I pleaded above, the mystery, the temptation to be other than I am disciplines me. Playing the role of a character I am not, and in most circumstances would not wish to be, renders me hyperalert. Pumps me up, and maybe I'm most myself not playing myself.

Please. If you believe nothing else about me, please believe I'm struggling for other words, my own words, even if they seem to spiral out of a mind, a mouth, like the driver's, my words, words I'm trying to earn, words I'm bound to fall on like a sword if they fail me. In other words I understand what it's like to be a dark passenger and can't help passing on when I speak the truth of that truth. What I haven't done, and never will, is be him, a small, pale, scared hairy mammal surrounded by giant carnivores whose dark bodies are hidden by darkness my eyes can't penetrate, fierce predators asleep or maybe prowling just inches away and any move I make, the slightest twitch, shiver, sneeze, *fluup* it's my nature to produce, risks awakening them.

Imagine a person in the car that snowy night, someone at least as wired as the driver, someone as helplessly alert, eyes hooded, stocking-capped hair hidden by a stingy brim, someone who has watched night fall blackly and falling snow mound in drifts taller than the Studebaker along fences bordering the highway, imagine this someone watching the driver, trying to piece together from the driver's movements and noises a picture of what the man at the wheel is thinking. Maybe the watcher's me, fresh from the Minneapolis conference, attempting to paint a picture of another's invisible thoughts. Or perhaps I'm still in my lime chair inventing a car-chase scene. You can't tell much by studying my face. A player's face disciplined to disguise my next move. Player or not, how can you be sure what someone else is thinking. Or seeing. Or saying. A different world inside each and every head, but we also like to believe another world's in there, a reasonably reliable facsimile of a reality we agree upon and pursue, a world the same for everyone, even though no one has been there or knows for sure if it's there. Who knows. Stories pretend to know. Stories claiming to be true. Not true. Both. Neither. Claiming to be inside and outside. Real and unreal. Stories swirling like the howling, savage storm pounding the Studebaker. Meaning what. Doesn't meaning always sit like Hinckley, nestled in darkness beyond the steamed peephole, meaning already sorted, toe-tagged, logged, an accident waiting for us to happen.

Since I've already violated Poe's rules for inventing stories,

I'll confess this fake Studebaker's interior is a site suspiciously like the inside of whatever kind of car my first coach, John Cinicola, drove back in the day when he chauffeured us, the Shadyside Boys Club twelve-and-under hoop team, to games around Pittsburgh, Pennsylvania, fifty years ago, when *fluups* not necessarily warnings of a bad heart or failing motor but farts, muted and discreet as possible in the close quarters of anywhere from seven to ten boy bodies crammed in for the ride, farts almost involuntary yet unavoidable, scrunched up as our intestines needed to be to fit in the overpacked car. Last suppers of beans and wieners didn't help. Fortunately, we shared the same low-rent, subsistence diet and our metabolisms homogenized the odor of the sneaky, invisible pellets of gas nobody could help expelling, grit your teeth, squirm, squeeze your sphincter as you might. Might as well ask us to stop breathing or snoring. Collectively we produced a foul miasma that would have knocked you off your feet if you were too close when the Studebaker's doors flung open in Hinckley, but the smell no big deal if you'd made the trip from Chicago's South Side. A thunderhead of bad air, but our air, it belonged to us, we bore it, as we bear our history, our culture, just as everybody else must bear theirs.

In other words stone funky inside the car, and when the driver cracks the window to cop a hit of fresh air, he's lying if he says he ain't mixed up in the raunchiness with the rest of us. Anyway not much happening in the single-wagon wagon train crossing barren flatlands west of Chicago, its pale canvas cover flapping like a berserk sail, the ship yawing, slapped and bruised by roaring waves that crest the bow, blinding surges of spray, foamy fingers of sea scampering like mice into the vessel's every nook and cranny. A monumental assault, but it gets old after a while, even though our hearts pump madly and our throats constrict and bowels loosen, after a while it's the same ole, same ole splish-splash whipping, ain't it so, my sisters and brothers and we steel ourselves to outlast the storm's lashing, nod off till it whips itself out. Thus we're not really missing much if we break another rule and flash forward to Hinckley.

One Hinckley resident in particular anxiously awaits our arrival. A boy named Rastus whose own arrival in town is legendary. They say his mama, a hoboing ho like those Scottsboro girls, so the story goes, landed in Hinckley just before her son. Landed butt first and busted every bone in her body when the flatcar she'd hopped, last car of a mile-long bluesy freight train, zigged when she thought it would zag, whipping her off her feet, tossing her ass over elbows high in the air. Miraculously, the same natural-born talent that transforms Negroes into skywalkers and speed burners enabled this lady to regain her composure while airborne and drop like an expertly flipped flapjack flat on her back. In spite of splitting her skull wide open and spilling brain like rotten cantaloupe all over the concrete platform of Hinckley station, her Fosbury flop preserved the baby inside her. Little Rastus, snug as a bug on the rug of his mama's prodigiously padded booty, sustained only minor injuries — a slight limp, a lisp, a sleepy IQ.

Poor orphaned Rastus didn't talk much and didn't exactly walk nor think straight either, but the townsfolk took pity on the survivor. Maybe they believed the good luck of his sunny-side-up arrival might rub off, because they passed him house to house until he was nine years old, old enough to earn his keep in the world, too old to play doctor and nurse in back yards with the town's daughters. Grown-up Rastus a familiar sight in Hinckley, chopping, hauling, sweeping. A hired boy you paid with scraps from the table. Rastus grateful for any kind of employment and pretty reliable too if you didn't mind him plodding along at his lazy pace. Given half a chance, Rastus could do it all. If somebody had invented fast-food joints in those days, Rastus might have aspired to assistant-manage one. Rastus, Hinckley's pet. Loved and worked like a dog. No respect, no pussy, and nothing but the scarecrow rags on his back he could really call his own, but Rastus only thirty-six. There's still time. Time Rastus didn't begin to count down until the Tuesday he saw on a pole outside Hinckley's only barbershop a flyer announcing the Harlem Globies' visit.

Of course Rastus couldn't read. But he understood what everybody else in town understood. The poster meant niggers coming. Maybe the word *Harlem,* printed in big letters across the top of the poster, exuded some distinctive ethnic scent, or maybe if you put your ear close to the poster you'd hear faint echoes of syncopated jazz, the baffled foot-tapping of Darktown strutters like ocean sound in seashells. Absent these clues, folks still get the point. The picture on the flyer worth a thousand words. And if other illiterates (the majority) in Hinckley understood immediately who was coming to town, why not Rastus. He's Hinckley if anybody's Hinckley. What else was he if he wasn't.

Rastus gazes raptly at the players on the flyer. He's the ugly duckling in the fairy tale discovering swans. Falls in love with the impossibly long, dark men, their big feet, big hands, big white lips, big white eyes, big, shiny white smiles, broad spade noses just like his. Falls in love with himself. Frowns recalling the day his eyes strayed into a mirror and the dusty glass revealed how different from other Hinckley folks he looked. Until the mirror sneaked up, *Boo,* he had avoided thinking too much about what other people saw when they looked at him. Mostly people had seemed not to look. Or they looked through him. Occasionally someone's eyes would panic as if they'd seen the devil. But Rastus saw devils and beasts too. The world full of them, so he wasn't surprised to see the scary sign of one still sticking like a fly to flypaper on somebody's eyeballs.

After the mirror those devilish beasts and beastly devils horned in everywhere. For instance, in the blue eyes of soft-limbed, teasing girls who'd turn his joint to a fiery stone, then prance away giggling. He learned not to look too closely. Learned to look away, look away. Taught himself to ignore his incriminating image when it floated across fragments of glass or the surface of still puddles, or inside his thoughts sometimes, tempting him to drown and disappear in glowing beast eyes that might be his. Hiding from himself no cure, however. Hinckley eyes penetrated his disguise. Eyes chewing and swallowing or spitting him out wet and mangled. Beast eyes no matter how artfully the bearer shapeshifted, fooled you with fleshy wrappings make your mouth water.

Maybe a flashback will clarify further why Rastus is plagued by a negative self-image. One day at closing time his main employer, Barber Jones, had said, You look like a wild man from Borneo, boy. All you need's a bone through your nose you ready for the circus. Set down the broom and get your tail over here to the mirror, boy. Ima show you a wild cannibal.

See yourself, boy. Look hard. See them filthy naps dragging down past your shoulders. People getting scared of you. Who you think you is. Don King or somebody. Damned wool stinks worse'n a skunk. Ima do you a favor, boy.

Barber Jones yakkety-yakking as he yaks daily about the general state of the world, the state of Hinckley and his dick first thing in the morning or last thing at night when just the two of them in the shop. Yakkety-yak, only now the subject is Rastus, not the usual nonstop monologue about rich folks in charge who were seriously fucking up, not running the world, nor Hinckley, nor his love life, the way Barber Jones would run things if just once he held the power in his hands, him in charge instead of those blockheads who one day will come crawling on their knees begging him to straighten things out, yakking and stropping on the razor strop a Bowie knife he'd brought special from home for this special occasion, an occasion Rastus very quickly figures he wants no part of, but since he's been a good boy his whole life, he waits, heart thumping like a tom-tom, beside a counter-to-ceiling mirror while fat-mouth Jones sharpens his blade.

A scene from Herman Melville's *Benito Cereno* might well have flashed through Rastus's mind if he'd been literate. But neither the African slave Babo shaving Captain Delano nor the ironic counterpoint of that scene, blackface and whiteface reversed, playing here in the mirror of Jones Barbershop, tweaks Rastus's consciousness of who he is and what's happening to him. Mr. Melville's prescient yarn doesn't creep into the head of Barber Jones either, even though Rastus pronounces "Barber" as *baba,* a sound so close to *Babo* it's a dead giveaway. Skinning knife in hand, Baba Jones is too busy stalking his prey, improvising Yankee-Doodle-like on the fly how in the hell he's going to scalp this coon and keep his hands clean. He snatches a towel from the soiled pile on the floor. He'll grab the bush with the towel, squeeze it in his fist, chop through the thick, knotty locks like chopping cotton.

Look at yourself in the mirror, boy. This the way you want to go round looking. Course it ain't. And stop your shakin. Ain't gon hurt you. You be thanking me once I'm done. Hell, boy, won't even charge you for a trim.

Lawd, lawd, am I truly dat nappy-haired ting in de mere. Am dat my bery own self, dat ugly ole pestering debil what don look lak nobody in Hinckley sides me. Is you me, Rastus. Lawd, lawd, you sho nuff tis me, Rastus confesses, confronting the living proof, his picture reversed right to left, left to right in the glass. Caged in the mirror like a prisoner in a cell is what he thinks, though not precisely in those words, nor does he think the word *panopticon,* clunkily Melvillean and thus appropriate for the network of gazes pinning him down to the place where they want him to stay. No words necessary to shatter the peace in Rastus's heart, to upset the détente of years of not looking, years of imagining himself more or less like other folks, just a slightly deformed, darker duck than the other ducks floating on this pond he'd learned to call Hinckley.

Boom. A shotgun blasts inside Rastus's brain, cold as the icy jolt when the driver cracks the Studebaker's window, as cold and maybe as welcome too, since if you don't wake up, Rastus, sleep can kill you. *Boom.* Every scared Hinckley duck quacks and flutters and scolds as it rises from the pond and leaves Rastus behind, very much alone. He watches them form neat, V-shaped squadrons high in the blue empyrean, squawking, honking, off to bomb the shit out of somebody in another country. You should have known long ago, should have figured it would happen like this one day. You all alone. Your big tarbaby feet in miring clay. You ain't them and they ain't you. Birds of a different feather. You might mistake them for geese flying in formation way up in the sky, but you sure ain't never heard them caw-caw, boy. Huh-uh. You the cawing bird and the shotgun aimed for you ain't gon miss next time. Your cover's busted, boy. Here come Baba Jones.

You sure don wanna go around looking just so, do you boy.

Well, Rastus ain't all kinds of fool. He zip-coons outta there, faster than a speeding bullet. (Could this be *it* — not the instant the jump shot is invented, we know better than that, but one of many moments, each monumental, memorable in its own way, when Rastus or whoever chooses to take his or her game up another level — not a notch but a quantum leap, higher, hyper, hipper — decides to put air under her or his feet, jumpshoot-jumpstart-rise-transcend, eschew the horizontal for the vertical, operating like Frantz Fanon when he envisioned a new day, a new plane of existence, a new reality, up, up, and away.) Maybe he didn't rise and fly, but he didn't Jim Crow neither. No turning dis way and wheeling dat way and jiggling up and down in place. Next time the baba seen him, bright and early a couple mornings later, Rastus had shaved his skull clean as a whistle. Gold chains draping his neck like Isaac Hayes. How Rastus accomplished such a transformation is another story, but we got enough stories by the tail feathers, twisted up in our white towel — count 'em — so let's switch back to the moment earlier in the story, later in Hinckley time, months after Rastus clipped his own wings rather than play Samson to Jones's Delilah.

Rastus still stands where we left him, hoodooed by the Harlem Globies' flyer. Bald, chained Rastus who's been nowhere. Doesn't even know what name his mother intended for him. Didn't even recognize his own face in the mirror till just yesterday, Hinckley time. Is the flyer a truer mirror than the one in the barbershop, the mirror Rastus assiduously keeps at his back these days as he sweeps, dusts, mops. He studies the grinning black men on the poster, their white lollipop lips, white circles around their eyes, white gloved fingers, his gaze full of longing, nostalgia, more than a small twinge of envy and regret. He doesn't know the Globies ain't been nowhere neither, not to Harlem nor nowhere else, their name unearned, ironic at this point in time. Like the jump shot, the Globies not quite invented yet. Still a gleam in the owner/driver's eye, his wishful thinking of international marketing, product endorsements, movies, TV cartoon, prodigious piles of currency, all colors, sizes, shapes promiscuously stacking up. Not Globies yet because this is the team's maiden voyage, first trot, first road game, this trek from Chicago to Hinckley. But they're on their way, almost here, if you believe the signs tacked and glued all over town, a rain, a storm, a blizzard of signs. If he weren't afraid the flimsy paper would come apart in his hands, Rastus would peel the flyer off the pole, sneak it into the barbershop, hold it up alongside his face so he could grin into the mirror with his lost brothers. Six Globies all in a row. Because, yes, in spite of signs of the beast, the players are like him. Different and alike. Alike and different. The circle unbroken. Yes. Yes. Yes. And *whoopee* they're coming to town.

Our boy Rastus sniffs opportunity knocking and decides — with an alacrity that would have astounded the townsfolk — to become a Globie and get the hell out of Hinckley.

As befits a fallen world, however, no good news travels without bad. The night of the game Rastus not allowed in the armory. Hinckley a northern town, so no Jim Crow laws turned Rastus away. Who needed a law to regulate the only Negro in town. Sorry, Rastus, just white folks tonight.

I neglected to mention an incident that occurred the year before Rastus dropped into Hinckley. The town's one little burnt-cork, burnt-matchstick tip of a dead-end street housing a few hard-luck Negroes had been spontaneously urban-removed, and its inhabitants, those who survived the pogrom, had disappeared into the night, the same kind of killingly cold night roughing up the Studebaker. That detail, the sudden exodus of all the town's Negroes, should have been noted earlier in story time, because it helps you understand Hinckley time. A visitor to Hinckley today probably won't hear about the above-mentioned event, yet it's imprinted indelibly in the town's memory. Now you see it, now you don't, but always present. A permanent marker separating before and after. Hinckley truly a white man's town from that night on.

And just to emphasize how white they wanted their town to be, the night of the fires everybody wore sheets bleached white as snow, and for a giggle, under the sheets, blacked their faces. A joke too good to share with the Negroes, who saw only white robes and white hoods with white eyes in the eyeholes. We blacked up blacker than the blackest of 'em, reported one old-timer in a back issue of the Hinckley *Daily News*. Yes we did. Blacker than a cold, black night, blacker than black. Hauled the coloreds outdoors in their drawers and nightgowns, pickaninnies naked as the day they born. Told 'em, You got five minutes to pack a sack and git. Five minutes we's turnin these shacks and everythin in 'em to ash.

Meanwhile the wagons transporting the Globies into town have arrived, their canvas covers billowing, noisy as wind-whipped sails, their wooden sides, steep as clipper ships, splashed with colorful, irresistible ads for merchandise nobody in Hinckley has ever dreamed of, let alone seen. A cornucopia of high-tech goods and services from the future, Hinckley time, though widely available in leading metropolitan centers for decades. Mostly beads and baubles, rummage-sale trash, but some stuff packed in the capacious holds of the wagons extremely ancient. Not stale or frail or old-fashioned or used or useless. No, the oldest, deepest cargo consisted of things forgotten. *Forgotten?* Yes, forgotten. Upon which subject I would expand if I could, but forgotten means forgotten, doesn't it. Means lost. A category whose contents I'm unable to list or describe because if I could, the items wouldn't be forgotten. Forgotten things are really, really gone. Gone even if memories of them flicker, ghosts with more life than the living. Like a *Free Marcus* button you tucked in a drawer and lived the rest of your life not remembering it lay there, folded in a bloodstained head kerchief, until one afternoon as you're preparing to move the last mile into senior citizens' public housing and you must get rid of ninety-nine and nine-tenths percent of the junk you've accumulated over the years because the cubicle you're assigned in the high-rise isn't much larger than a coffin, certainly not a king-sized coffin like pharaohs erected so they could take everything with them — chariots, boats, VCRs, slaves, wives — so you must shed what feels like layers of your own tender skin, flaying yourself patiently, painfully, divesting yourself of one precious forgotten thing after another, toss, toss, toss. Things forgotten in the gritty bottom of a drawer and you realize you've not been living the kind of life you could have lived if you hadn't forgotten, and now, remembering, it's too late.

In other words, the wagons carried tons of alternative pasts — roads not taken, costumes, body parts, promises, ghosts. Hinckley folks lined up for miles at these canvas-topped depots crackling whitely in the prairie wind. Even poor folks who can't afford to purchase anything mob the landing, ooohing and ahhhing with the rest. So many bright lost hopes in the bellies of the schooners, the wagons might still be docked there doing brisk business a hundred years from now, the Globies in their gaudy, revealing uniforms showing their stuff to a sea of wide eyes, waving hands, grappling, grasping hands, but hands not too busy to clap, volleys of clapping, then a vast, collective sigh when clapping stops and empty hands drop to people's sides, sighs so deep and windy they scythe across the Great Plains, rippling mile after endless mile of wheat, corn, barley, amber fields of grain swaying and purring as if they'd been caressed when a tall Globie dangles aloft some item everybody recognizes, a forgotten thing all would claim if they could afford it, a priceless pearl the dark ballplayer tosses gratis into the crowd of Hinckleyites, just doing it to do it, and the gift would perform tricks, loop-de-looping, sparkling, airborne long enough to evoke spasms of love and guilt and awe and desire and regret, then disappear like a snowflake or a sentence grown too large and baroque, its own weight and ambition and daring and vanity ripping it apart before it reaches the earth. A forgotten thing twisting in the air, becoming a wet spot on fingers reaching for it. A tear inching down a cheek. An embarrassing drop of moisture in the crotch of somebody's drawers.

Wheee. Forgotten things. Floating through the air with the greatest of ease. Hang-gliding. Flip-flopping.

Flip-floppety-clippety-clop. The horse-drawn caravan clomps up and down Hinckley's skimpy grid of streets. Disappears when it reaches the abandoned, dead-end, former black quarter and turns right to avoid the foundation of a multiuse, multistory, multinational parking garage and amusement center, a yawning hole gouged deeper into the earth than the stainless steel and glass edifice will rise into the sky.

Is dat going to be the Mall of America, one of the Globie kids asks, peeking out from behind a wagon's canvas flap. A little Hinckley girl hears the little Globie but doesn't reply.

Then she's bright and chirrupy as Jiminy Cricket and

chases after the gillies till she can't keep up, watching the last horse's round, perfect rump swaying side to side like Miss Maya's verse. Feels delicious about herself because she had smiled, managed to be polite to the small brown face poking out of the white sheet just as her mother said she must, but also really, basically, ignored it, didn't get the brown face mixed up with Hinckley faces her mother said it wouldn't and couldn't ever be. Always act a lady, honey. But be careful. Very careful. Those people are not like us. Warmed by the boy's soft voice, his long eyelashes like curly curtains or question marks, the dreamy roll of the horse's huge, split butt, but she didn't fall in love. Instead she chatters to herself in a new language, made up on the spot. *Wow. Gumby-o. Kum-bye-a. Op-poop-a-doop* . . . as if she's been tossed a forgotten thing and it doesn't melt.

She wishes she'd said yes to the boy, wishes she could share the good news.

Daddy said after the bulldozers a big road's coming, sweety-pie, and we'll be the centerpiece of the universe, the envy of our neighbors, Daddy said I can have anything I want, twenty-four seven, brother, just imagine, anything I want, cute jack-in-the-box, pop-up brown boys, a pinto pony, baby dolls with skin warm and soft as mine, who cry real tears. *Word. Bling-bling. Oop-poop-a-doop.*

After a dust cloud churned by the giant tires of the convoy settles, the little girl discovers chocolate drops wrapped in silver foil the chocolate soldiers had tossed her. In the noise and confusion of the rumbling vehicles, she'd thought the candies were stones. Or cruel bullets aimed at her by the dark strangers in canvas-roofed trucks her mother had warned her to flee from, hide from. Realizing they are lovely chocolate morsels, immaculate inside their shiny skins, she feels terrible for thinking ugly thoughts about the GIs, wants to run to the convoy and say *Danke, Danke* even though her mother told her, They're illiterate, don't speak our language. As she scoops up the surprises and stuffs them in her apron pocket, she imagines her chubby legs churning in pursuit of the dusty column. The convoy had taken hours to pass her, so it must be moving slowly. But war has taught her the treacherous distance between dreams and reality. Even after crash diets and aerobic classes her pale short legs would never catch the wagons, so she sits down, settles for cramming food into her mouth with both hands, as if she's forgotten how good food can be and wants to make up for all the lost meals at once. Licking, sucking, crunching, chewing. The melting, gooey drops smear her cheeks, hands, dimpled knees—chocolate stain spreading as the magic candy spawns, multiplies inside her apron pocket, a dozen new sweet pieces explode into being for every piece she consumes. She eats till she's about to bust, sweet chocolate coating her inside and out, a glistening, sticky tarbaby her own mother would have warned her not to touch. Eats till she falls asleep and keels over in the dusty street.

Dusty? What's up with this dusty. I thought you said it was snowing. A snowstorm.

Snowstorm. Oh yeah. Should have let you know that in expectation of a four-seasons mega–pleasure center, Hinckley domed itself last year.

Believe it or not, it's Rastus who discovers the girl. Since being refused entrance to the Globies' show, he's been wandering disconsolate through Hinckley's dark streets when suddenly, as fate would have it, he stumbles into her. Literally. Ouch.

Less painful than unnerving when Rastus makes abrupt contact with something soft and squishy underfoot. He freezes in his tracks. Instinctively his leg retracts. He scuffs the bottom of his shoe on the ground, remembering the parade earlier in the day, horses large as elephants. Sniffs the night air cautiously. Hopes he's wrong. Must be. He smells sugar and spice, everything nice, overlaid with the cloyingly sweet reek of chocolate.

Another time and place he might have reared back, kicked the obstacle in his path, but tonight he's weak, depleted, the mean exclusion of him from the Globie extravaganza the final straw. Besides, what kind of person would kick a dog already down, and dog or cat's what he believes he'll see as he peers into the shadows webbing his feet.

Rastus gulps. His already overtaxed heart *fluups*. Chocolate can't hide a cherub's face, the Gerber baby plump limbs and roly-poly torso. Somebody's daughter lying out here in the gutter. Hoodooed. Stricken. Poor babygirl. Her frail — make up your mind — chest rises and falls faintly, motion almost imperceptible since they never installed streetlamps on this unpaved street when Negroes lived here, and now the cunning city managers are waiting for the Dutch-German-Swiss conglomerate to install a megawatt, mesmerizing blaze of glory to guide crowds to the omniplex.

Believe it or not, on this night of nights, this night he expected a new life to begin, riding off with the Globies, the players exhausted but hungry for another town tomorrow, laughing, telling lies, picking salty slivers of the town they've just sacked out their teeth, on this penultimate night before the dawning of the first day of his new life, Rastus displays patience and self-denial worthy of Harriet's Tom. Accepts the sudden turn of fate delaying his flight from Hinckley. Takes time out to rescue a damsel in distress.

One more job, just one more and I'm through, outta here. Trotting with the Globies or flying on my own two feet, I'm gittin out. Giddy-up. Yeah. Tell folks it was Rastus singing dis sad song, now Rastus up and gone.

Determined to do the right thing, he stoops and raises the girl's cold, heart-shaped face, one large hand under her neck so her head droops backward and her mouth flops open, the other hand flat against her tiny bosom. Figures he'll blow breath into her mouth, then pump her ribcage like you would a bellows till her lungs catch fire again. In other words Rastus is inventing CPR, cardiopulmonary resuscitation, a lifesaving technique that will catch on big in America one day in the bright future when hopefully there will be no rules about who can do it to whom, but that night in Hinckley, well, you can imagine what happened when a crowd of citizens hopped up and confused by Globie shenanigans at the armory came upon Rastus in the shadows crouched over a bloody, unconscious little white girl, puckering up his big lips to deliver a kiss.

To be fair, not everyone participated in the mayhem you're imagining. Experts say the portion of the crowd returning home to the slum bordering the former colored quarter must shoulder most of the blame. In other words, the poor and fragrant did the dirty work. The ones who live where no self-respecting white person would, an unruly element, soon themselves to be evicted when Consolidated Enterprises clears more parking space for the pleasure center, the same people, experts say, who had constituted by far the largest portion of the mob that had burned and chased all the Negroes out of town, these embarrassing undesirables and unemployables, who would lynch foreign CEOs too if they could get away with it, are responsible, experts will explain, for perpetrating the horror I'm asking you to imagine. And imagine you must, because I refuse to regale you with gory, unedifying details.

Clearly, not everyone's to blame. Certainly not me or you. On the other hand, who wouldn't be upset by an evening of loud, half-naked, large black men fast breaking and fancy dribbling, clowning and stuffing and jamming and preening for white women and kids screaming their silly heads off. Enough to put any grown man's nerves on edge, especially after you had to shell out your hard-earned cash to watch yourself take a beating. Then, to top it all off, once you're home, bone tired, hunkered down on your side of the bed, here comes your old lady grinning from ear to ear, bouncy like she's just survived a naked bungy-dive from the top of the goddamned pleasure center's twin-towers-to-be.

The Studebaker's wipers flop back and forth, bump over scabs of ice. The driver's view isn't improving. We inch along a long, long black tunnel, headlights illuminating slants of snow that converge just a few yards beyond the spot where a hood ornament would sit, if Studebakers, like Mercedes Benzes, were adorned with bowsprits in 1927. Bright white lines of force, every kamikaziing snowflake in the universe sucked into this vortex, this vanishing point the headlights define, a hole in the dark we chug, chug behind, the ever receding horizon drawing us on, drawing us on, a ship to Zion, the song says.

Our driver's appalled by the raw deal Rastus received. During an interview he asserts, I'd never participate in something so mobbishly brutal. I would not assume appearance is reality. I would never presume truth lodges in the eyes of the more numerous beholders. After all, my people also a minority. We've suffered unjustly too. And will again. I fear it in my bones. Soon after the great depression that will occur just a few years from now, just a few miles down this very road we're traveling in this hot, *fluup*ing car, some clever, evil motherfucker will say, Sew yellow stars on their sleeves. Stars will work like color. We'll be able to tell who's who. Protect our citizens from mongrels, gypsies, globetrotters, migrants, emigrants, the riffraff coming and going. Sneaking in and out of our cities. Peddling dangerous wares. Parasites. Criminals. Terrorists. Devils.

Through the slit in his iron mask the driver observes gallows being erected by the roadside. Imagines flyers nailed and taped all over town. Wonders if it had been wise to warn them we're coming.

So *who* invented the jump shot. Don't despair. All the panelists have taken seats facing the audience. The emcee at the podium taps a microphone and a hush fills the vast hall. We're about to be told.

What We Cannot Speak About We
Must Pass Over in Silence

I HAVE A FRIEND with a son in prison. About once a year he
visits his son. Since the prison is in Arizona and my friend
lives here on the East Coast, visiting isn't easy. He's told me the
planning, the expense, the long day spent flying there and
longer day flying back are the least of it. The moment that's not
easy, that's impossible, he said, is after three days, six hours
each, of visiting are over and he passes through the sliding gate
of the steel-fenced outdoor holding pen between the prison visitation compound and the visitors' parking lot and steps onto
the asphalt that squirms beneath your feet, oozing hot like it
just might burn through your shoe soles before you reach the
rental car and fling open its doors and blast the air conditioner
so the car's interior won't fry your skin, it's then, he said, taking
your first steps away from the prison, first steps back into the
world, when you almost come apart, almost lose it completely
out there in the desert, emptiness stretching as far as the eye can
see, very far usually, ahead to a horizon ironed flat by the weight
of blue sky, to the right and left zigzag mountain peaks marking
the edges of the earth, nothing moving but hot air wiggling
above the highway, the scrub brush and sand, then, for an un-
ending instant, it's very hard to be alive, he says, and thinks he
doesn't want to live a minute longer and would not make it to
the car, the airport, back to this city if he didn't pause and remind himself it's worse, far worse for the son behind him still
trapped inside the prison, so for the son's sake he manages a

first step away, then another and another. In these faltering moments he must prepare himself for the turnaround, the jarring transition into a world where he has no access to his son except for rare ten-minute phone calls, a blighted world he must make sense of again, beginning with the first step away and back through the boiling caldron of parking lot, first step of the trip that will return him in a year to the desert prison.

Now he won't have it to worry about anymore. When I learned of the friend's death, I'd just finished fixing a peanut butter sandwich. Living alone means you tend to let yourself run out of things. Milk, dishwasher detergent, napkins, toothpaste — staples you must regularly replace. At least it happens to me. In this late bachelorhood with no live-in partner who shares responsibility for remembering to stock up on needful things. Peanut butter a choice I didn't relish, but probably my only choice that evening, so I'd fixed one, or two, more likely, since they'd be serving as dinner. In the day's mail I'd ignored till I sat down to my sorry-assed meal, a letter from a lawyer announcing the death of the friend with a son in prison, and inside the legal-sized manila envelope a sealed white envelope the friend had addressed to me.

I was surprised on numerous counts. First, to learn the friend was gone. Second, to find he'd considered me significant enough to have me informed of his passing. Third, the personal note. Fourth, and now it's time to stop numbering, no point since you could say every event following the lawyer's letter both a surprise and no surprise, so numbering them as arbitrary as including the sluggish detail of peanut butter sandwiches, "sluggish" because I'd become intrigued by the contents of the manila envelope and stopped masticating the wad in my jaw until I recalled the friend's description of exiting prison, and the sludge became a mouthful of scalding tar.

What's surprising about death anyway, unless you count the details of when and how, the precise violence stopping the heart, the volume of spilled blood, those unedifying, uninformative details the media relentlessly flog as news. Nothing really surprising about death except how doggedly we insist on being surprised by what we know very well's inevitable, and of course, after a while, this insistence itself unsurprising. So I was (a) surprised and (b) not surprised by the death of a friend who wasn't much of a friend, after all, more acquaintance than intimate cut-buddy, a guy I'd met somewhere through someone and weeks later we'd recognized each other in a line at a movie or a bank and nodded and then ran into each other again one morning in a busy coffeeshop and since I'm partial to the coffee there, I did something I never do, asked if it was okay to share his table and he smiled and said sure so we became in this sense friends. I never knew very much about him and hadn't known him very long. He never visited my apartment nor I his. A couple years of casual bump-ins, tables shared for coffee while we read our newspapers, a meal, a movie or two, a playoff game in a bar once, two middle-aged men who live alone and inhabit a small, self-sufficient corner of a large city and take time-outs here and there from living alone so being alone at this stage in our careers doesn't feel too depressingly like loneliness. The same motivation, same pattern governing my relationships with the occasional woman who consents to share my bed or if she doesn't consent to sleep with me entertains the option long enough, seriously enough, with attitudes interesting enough to keep us distracted by each other for a while.

Reconsidering the evening I received notice of the friend's death, going over my reactions again, putting words to them, I realize I'm underplaying my emotions. Not about the shock or sadness of losing the friend. He's the kind of person you could see occasionally, enjoy his company more or less, and walk away with no further expectations, no plan to meet again. If he'd moved to another city, months might have passed before I'd notice him missing. If we'd lost contact for good, I'm sure I wouldn't have regretted not seeing him. A smidgen of curiosity, perhaps. Perhaps a slight bit of vexation, as when I discover I haven't restocked paper towels or Tabasco sauce. Less, since his absence wouldn't leave a gap I'd be obliged to fill. My usual flat response at this stage in my life to losing things I have no power to hold on to. Most of the world fits into this category now, so what I'm trying to say is that something about the manila envelope and its contents bothered me more than I'm used to allowing things to bother me, though I'm not sure why. Was it the son in prison. The friend had told me no one else visited. The son's mother dead of cancer. Her people, like the friend's, like mine, old, scattered, gone. Another son, whereabouts unknown, who'd disowned his father and half-brother, started a new life somewhere else. I wondered if the lawyer who wrote me had been instructed to inform the son in prison of his father's passing. How were such matters handled. A phone call. A registered letter. Maybe a visit from the prison chaplain. I hoped my friend had arranged things to run smoothly, with as little distress as possible for the son. Any alternatives I imagined seemed cruel. Cruel for different reasons, but equally difficult for the son. Was he even now opening his manila envelope, a second envelope tucked inside with its personal message. I guess I do know why I was upset—the death of the man who'd been my acquaintance for nearly two years moved me not a bit, but I grieved to the point of tears for a son I'd never seen, never spoken to, who probably wasn't aware my grief or I existed.

Empathy for the son not surprising, even logical, under the circumstances, you might say. Why worry about the father. He's gone. No more tiptoeing across burning coals. Why not sympathize with a young man suddenly severed from his last living contact with the world this side of prison bars. Did he know his father wouldn't be visiting. Had the son phoned. Listened to it ring-ring-ring and ring. How would he find out. How would he bear the news.

Of course I considered the possibility that my reaction or overreaction might be a way of feeling sorry for myself. For the sorry, running-down-to-the-ground arc all lives eventually assume. Sorry for the prison I've chosen to seal myself within. Fewer and fewer visits paid or received. No doubt a bit of self-pity colored my response. On the other hand I'm not a brooder. I quickly become bored when a mood's too intense or lasts too long. Luckily, I have the capacity to step back, step away, escape into a book, a movie, a vigorous walk, and if these distractions don't do the trick, then very soon I discover I'm smiling, perhaps even quietly chuckling at the ridiculous antics of the person who's lost control, who's taking himself and his commonplace dilemmas far too seriously.

> Dear Attorney Koppleman,
>
> I was a friend of the late Mr. Donald Williams. You wrote to inform me of Mr. Williams's death. Thank you. I'm trying to reach Mr. Williams's imprisoned son to offer my belated condolences. If you possess the son's mailing address, could you pass it on to me, please. I appreciate in advance your attention to this matter.

♦ ♦ ♦

> In response to your inquiry of 6/24/99: this office did execute Mr. Donald K. Williams's will. The relevant documents have been filed in Probate Court, and as such are part of the public record you may consult at your convenience.
>
> P.S. Wish I could be more helpful but in our very limited dealings with Mr. Williams, he never mentioned a son in or out of prison.

I learned there are many prisons in Arizona. Large and small. Local, state, federal. Jails for short stays, penitentiaries for lifers. Perhaps it's the hot, dry climate. Perhaps space is cheap.

Perhaps a desert state's economy, with limited employment opportunities for its citizens, relies on prisons. Perhaps corporate-friendly deals make prisons lucrative businesses. Whatever the reasons, the prison industry seems to flourish in Arizona. Many people also wind up in Arizona retirement communities. Do the skills accumulated in managing the senior citizens who come to the state to die readily translate to prison administration, or vice versa. I'm dwelling on the number of prisons only because it presented a daunting obstacle as I began to search for the late friend's son.

Fortunately, the state employs people to keep track of prisoners. I'm not referring to uniformed guards charged with hands-on monitoring of inmate flesh and blood. I mean computer people who know how to punch in and retrieve information. Are they one of the resources attracting prisons to Arizona. Vast emptiness plus a vast legion of specialists adept at processing a steady stream of bodies across borders, orchestrating the dance of dead and living so vacancies are filled and fees collected promptly, new residents recruited, old ones disposed of. Was it the dead friend who told me the downtown streets of Phoenix are eerily vacant during heatstroke daylight hours. People who do the counting must be sequestered in air-conditioned towers or busy as bees underground in offices honeycombed beneath the asphalt, their terminals regulating traffic in and out of hospices, prisons, old folks' homes, juvenile detention centers, cemeteries, their screens displaying Arizona's archipelago of incarceral facilities, diagrams of individual gulags where a single speck with its unique, identifying tag can be pinpointed at any moment of the day. Thanks to such a highly organized system, after much digging I located the son.

Why did I search. While I searched, I never asked why. Most likely because I expected no answer. Still don't. Won't fake one now except to suggest (a) curiosity and (b) anger. Curiosity since I had no particular agenda beyond maybe sending a card or note. The search pure in this sense, an experiment, driven by the simple urge to know. Curiosity motivating me like it drove the proverbial cat, killing it until satisfaction brought it back. Anger because I learned how perversely the system functions, how slim your chances of winning are if you challenge it.

Anger because the system's insatiable clockwork innards had the information I sought and refused to divulge it. Refused fiercely, mindlessly, as only a mindless machine created to do a single, repetitive, mindless task can mindlessly refuse. The prison system assumes an adversarial stance the instant an inquiry attempts to sidestep the prerecorded labyrinth of logical menus that protect its irrational core. When and if you ever reach a human voice, its hostile tone insinuates you've done something stupid or morally suspect by pursuing it to its lair. As punishment for your trespass, the voice will do its best to mimic the tone and manner of the recorded messages you've been compelled to suffer in order to reach it.

Anger, because I couldn't help taking the hassle personally. Hated equally the bland bureaucratic sympathy or disdain or deafness or defensiveness or raw, aggressive antagonism, the multiplicity of attitudes and accents live and recorded transmitting exactly the same bottom-line message: yes, what you want I have, but I'm not parting with it easily.

I won't bore you or myself by reciting how many times I was put on hold or switched or switched back or the line went dead after hours of Muzak or I weathered various catch-22 routines. I'll just say I didn't let it get the best of me. Swallowed my anger, and with the help of a friend, persevered, till one day — accidentally, I'm sure — the information I'd been trying to pry from the system's grip collapsed like an escaping hostage into my arms.

> I'm writing to express my condolences sympathies
> upon the death of your father at the death of your father
> your father's passing though I was barely acquainted

only superficially I'm writing to you because I was a friend of your father by now prison officials must have informed you of his death his demise the bad news I assume I don't want to intrude on your grief sorrow privacy if in fact hadn't known your sorrow and the circumstances of our lives known him very long only a few years permitted allowed only limited opportunities to become acquainted and the circumstances of our lives I considered your father a friend I can't claim to know him your father well but our paths crossed often frequently I considered him a good valuable friend fine man I was very sorry to hear learn of his death spoke often of you on many occasions his words Please allow me to express my sympathy for your great loss I don't claim to know to have known him well but I your father fine man good man considered him a valuable friend heartfelt he spoke of you many times always quite much good love affection admiration I feel almost as if I you know you though I'm a complete stranger his moving words heartfelt about son compelled me to write this note if I can be helpful in any fashion manner if I can be of assistance in this matter at this difficult time place don't hesitate to let me know please don't

I was sorry to hear of your father's death. We were friends. Please accept my heartfelt regrets on this sad occasion.

◆　◆　◆

Some man must have fucked my mother. All I knew about him until your note said he's dead. Thanks.

It could have ended there. A case of mistaken identity. Or a lie. Or numerous lies. Or a hallucination. Or fabrication. Had I been duped. By whom. Father, son, both. Did they know each other or not. What did I know for sure about either one. What stake did I have in either man's story. If I connected the dots, would a picture emerge. One man dead, the other good as dead locked up two thousand miles away in an Arizona prison. Was any of it my business. Anybody's business.

I dress lightly, relying on the weather lady's promises.

A woman greets me and introduces herself as Suh Jung, Attorney Koppleman's paralegal. She's a tiny, pleasant Asian woman with jet-black hair brutally cropped above her ears, a helmet, she'll explain later, necessary to protect herself from the cliché of submissiveness, the china-doll stereotype people immediately applied when they saw a thick rope of hair hanging past her waist, hair her father insisted she not cut but wear twisted into a single braid in public, her mother combing, brushing, oiling her hair endlessly till shiny pounds of it were lopped off the day the father died and then, strangely, she'd wanted to save the hair she had hated, wanted to glue it back together strand by strand and drape it over one of those pedestaled heads you see in beauty shops so she and her mother could continue forever the grooming rituals that had been one of the few ways they could relate in a household her father relentlessly, meticulously hammered into an exquisitely lifelike, flawless representation of his will, like those sailing ships in bottles or glass butterflies in the museum, so close to the real thing you stare and stare waiting for them to flutter away, a household the father shattered in a fit of pique or rage or boredom the day she opened the garage door after school and found him barefoot, shitty-pantsed, dangling from a rafter beside the green family Buick.

In the lawyer's office she listened to my story about father and son, took notes carefully, it seemed, though her eyes were cool, a somewhere-else distracted cool while she performed her legal-assistant duties. Black, distant eyes framed in round, metal-rimmed, old-lady spectacles that belied the youthful freshness of her skin. Late at night when she'd talk about her dead father, I'd notice the coolness of the first day, and as I learned more about him — or rather, as I formed my own impression of him, since she volunteered few details, spoke instead about being a quiet, terrified girl trying to swim through shark-infested water without making waves — I guessed she had wanted to imitate the father's impenetrable gaze, practicing, practicing till she believed she'd gotten it right, but she didn't get it right, probably because she never understood the father's coldness, never made her peace with the blankness behind his eyes where she yearned to see her image take shape, where it never did, never would. Gradually I came to pity her, her unsuccessful theft of her father's eyes, her transparent attempt to conceal her timidity behind the father's stare, timidity I despised because it reminded me of mine, my inadequacies and half-measures and compromises, begging and fearing to be seen, my lack of directness, decisiveness, my deficiency of enterprise and imagination, manifested in her case by the theatrical gesture of chopping off her hair when confronted by the grand truth of her father's suicide. Timidity dooming her to cliché — staring off inscrutably into space.

Given her history, the lost-father business in my story must have teased out her curiosity. Otherwise, why would she take notice of me. Going by appearances — her pale, unlined face, my stern, dark, middle-aged mask — I was too old for her. I could suggest (a) she was older than she looked and (b) I'm younger than you might guess at first glance, but then I'd be hedging, suggesting some middle ground we shared almost as peers, and such turned out not to be the case. I wasn't old enough to be her father, but that dreadful plausibility enforced a formal distance between us, distance we maintained in public, distance that at first could be stimulating erotically, for me at least, until the necessity of denying difference, denying the evidence of my eyes, became less a matter of play than a chore, a discipline and duty, even when we were together in private.

Behind a desk almost comically dwarfing her (seeing it, I should have been alerted by its acres of polished blond wood to the limits, the impropriety of any intimacy we'd establish), she listened politely, eventually dissuaded me from what I'd anticipated as the object of my visit — talking to Attorney Koppleman. She affirmed her postscript: no one in the office knew anything about a son in prison. I thanked her, accepted the card she offered to substantiate her willingness to help in any way she could.

Would you like me to call around out in Arizona. At least save you some time, get you started in the right direction.

Thanks. That's very kind of you. But I probably need to do some thinking on this.

And then I realized how stupidly wishy-washy I must sound. It galled me, because I work hard to give just the opposite impression. Appear to be a man sure of himself, not the kind of jerk who bothers people, wasting their valuable time because he doesn't know what he wants. So perhaps that's why I flirted. Not flirted exactly, but asserted myself in the only way I could think of at the moment, by plainly, abruptly letting her see I was interested. In her. The woman part of her. A decisive act, yet suspect from the beginning, since it sprang from no particular spark of attraction. Still, a much more decisive move than I'm usually capable of making — true or false. Hitting on her, so to speak, straight up, hard, asking for the home number she hastily scribbled on the back of her card, hurrying as if she suddenly remembered a lineup of urgent tasks awaiting our interview's termination. Her way of attending to a slightly embarrassing necessity. The way some women I've met, and men too, I suppose, treat sex. Jotting down the number, she was as out of character as I was, but we pulled it off. A silly, halfhearted, doomed exchange in a downtown office, pulling it off in spite of ourselves. Me driven to retrieve dignity I was afraid I'd compromised. Her motive opaque, then as now. Even though the lost-father business leaps out at you, it doesn't account for her lifting her gaze from her cluttered desk, from the file on top of the pile on which she'd laid her card, staring at me, then dashing off her number on the back.

Thanks again. And thank you for this, I said, pressing my luck, nodding at the card I was holding back side up, my arm extended toward her, as if I were nearsighted and needed distance to read what she'd written, but she didn't raise her eyes again to the bait I dangled or she dangled or whatever it was either of us believed we were accomplishing in the lawyer's office that afternoon.

The world is full of remarkable things. Amiri Baraka penned those words when he was still LeRoi Jones writing his way back to Newark and a new name after a lengthy sojourn among artsy, crazy white folks in the Village. One of my favorite lines from one of my favorite writers. Back in the day when I still pretended books worth talking about, people were surprised to discover Baraka a favorite of mine, as quietly integrated and nonconfrontational a specimen as I seemed to be of America's longest, most violently reviled minority. It wasn't so much a matter of the quality of what Jones/Baraka had written as it was the chances he'd taken, chances in his art, in his life. Sacrifices of mind and body he endured so I could vicariously participate, safely holed up in my corner. Same lair where I sat out Vietnam, a college boy while my cousin and most guys from my high school were drafted, shot at, jailed, murdered, became drug addicts in a war raging here and abroad.

Remarkable things. With Suh Jung I smoked my first joint in years. At fifty-seven learned to bathe a woman and, what was harder, learned to relax in a tub while a woman bathed me. Contacting the son in prison not exactly on hold while she and I experienced low-order remarkable things. I knew which Arizona prison held him and had received from the warden's office the information I'd requested about visiting. Completing my business with this woman was a necessary step in the process of preparing myself for whatever I decided to do next. Steaming water, her soapy hands scrubbing my shoulders, cleansed me, fortified me. I shed old skins. When the son in prison set his eyes on me, I wanted to glow. If he saw me at my best, wouldn't he understand everything.

The dead friend my age more or less, so that could mean the son more or less Suh Jung's age. He should be the suitor. The shoulders she lathered, the hand stubbing out the roach in a mayonnaise jar cap, could be his. What would he see, turning to embrace the woman sitting up naked next to me in bed. She's small, boy-hipped, breasts slight pouches under long nipples that attract attention to an absence rather than presence they crown, twin sentry towers on her bony chest, guarding an outpost no aggressor's likely to target. Is she a woman the son would desire. What sort of woman does the son fantasize when he masturbates. What if the son awakened here, his cell transformed to this room, the son imprisoned here with this woman, sweet smoke settling in his lungs, mellowing him out after all the icy years. Me locked in the black Arizona night imagining a woman. Would it be the same woman in both places at once or different limbs, eyes, wetnesses, scents, like those tigers whirling about Sambo, tigers no longer tigers as they chase each other faster and faster, overwhelming poor little Sambo's senses, his Sambo black brain, as he tosses and turns in waking-sleep, a mixed-up colored boy, the coins his mother gave him clutched in a sweaty fist, trying once more to complete a simple errand and reach home in one piece.

Why would I be ashamed if caught with a woman who might be the age of the son rotting in prison. What difference to the son whether or not I have a lover or what her age might be. If I'm celibate till I die, would my abstinence buy him freedom one instant sooner. If my trip or possible trip's stalled while I dally with a woman, so what. I'm going to visit, not bring him home. What's wrong with sorting out my motivations, my ambivalence, calculating consequences. Always plenty to sort out, isn't there: fathers, sons, daughters, deaths, the proper care and feeding of the selfish, greedy animal each of us is, the desirability of short-lived affairs to distract us from the awful humiliations we're born to suffer aging and dying. I'm more alone now, fifty-seven years later, than when I arrived spanking brand-new on the planet. Instead of being delayed, my trip to Arizona is beginning here, being born here in this grappling, this tangle.

Have you written again.

No, just the once. His answer enough to cure me of letter writing forever.

But you say you're ready to visit. Do you have a ticket. Or are you going to stamp your forehead and mail yourself to Arizona.

The city bumps past, cut up through the bus windows. We had headed for the last row of seats in the back, facing the driver. Seats on the rear bench meant fewer passengers stepping over, around, on you during the long ride uptown to the museum. Fewer people leaning over you. Sneezing. Coughing. Eavesdropping. Fewer strangers boxing you in, saying stuff you don't want to hear but you find yourself listening anyway, the way you had watched in spite of yourself the never-turned-off TV set in your mother's living room. Fresh blood pooled on one of the butt-molded blue seats you intended to occupy. A wet, silver-dollar-sized fresh glob. You consider changing buses. Could you transfer without being double-fared. What about the good chance you'd hop from frying pan to fire, catch a bus with a raving maniac on board or a fleet of wheelchairs docking or undocking every other corner. Better to leave well enough alone. Take seats cattycorner from the bloody one. The blood's not going to jump the aisle and bite you. Fortunately, you noticed it before either of you splashed down in it. You check again, eyeballing one more time the blue seats you're poised above, looking for blood, expecting blood, as if blood's a constant danger though you've never seen blood before on a bus bumping from uptown to downtown, downtown to uptown in all the years of riding until this very day.

We almost missed the Giacometti.

Not there yet.

It closes next weekend.

Right on time, then. I'm away next week.

Oh, you're going to Arizona next week.

I've been letting other things get in the way. Unless I set a hard date, the visit won't happen. You know. Like we kept putting off Giacometti.

You booked a flight.

Not yet.

But you're going for sure. Next week.

I think so think so think so think so think so.

I loved the slinky dog. He was so . . . so . . . you know . . . *dog*. An alley-cat dog like the ones always upsetting the garbage cans behind my father's store. Stringy and scrawny like them. Swaybacked. Hunkered down like they're hiding or something's after them even when they're just pit-patting from place to place. Scruffy barbed-wire fur. Those long, floppy, flat dog feet like bedroom slippers.

To tell the truth, too much to see. I missed the dog. I was overwhelmed. By the crowd, the crowd of objects.

Two weeks after the Giacometti exhibit, I could make more sense of it. A fat, luxurious book by a French art critic helped. It cost so much I knew I'd force myself to read it, or at least study the copious illustrations. The afternoon in the MOMA I'd done more reading than looking at art. Two floors, numerous galleries, still it was like fighting for a handhold on a subway pole. Reading captions shut out the crowd. I could stand my ground without feeling the pressure of somebody behind me demanding a peek.

I wondered why Giacometti didn't go insane. Maybe he did. Even without the French critic I could sense Giacometti didn't trust what was in front of his eyes. He felt the strangeness, the menace. He understood art always failed. Art lied to him. People's eyes lied. No one ever sees the world as it is. Giacometti's eyes failed him too. He'd glance away from a model to the image of it he was making, he said, and when he looked back to check the model, it would be different, always different, always changing.

Frustrated by my inability to recall the dead friend's face, I twisted on the light over the mirror above the bathroom sink, thinking I might milk the friend's features from mine. Hadn't we been vaguely similar in age and color. If I studied hard, maybe the absence in my face of some distinctive trait the friend possessed would trigger my memory, or vice versa, a trait I bore would recall its absence in the friend's features, and bingo, his whole face would appear.

There is an odd neurological deficit that prevents some people from recognizing faces. Seeing the stranger in the mirror, I was afraid I might be suffering from the disorder. Who in God's name was this person. Who'd been punished with those cracks, blemishes, the mottled complexion, eyes sunk in deep hollows, frightened eyes crying out for acknowledgment, for help, then receding, surrendering, staring blankly, bewildered and exhausted, asking me the same questions I was asking them.

Rather than attempt to account for the wreckage, I began to repair the face, working backward, a makeup artist removing years from an actor, restoring a young man the mirror denied. How long had I been losing track of myself. Not really looking when I brushed my teeth or combed my hair, letting the image in the mirror soften and blur, become as familiar and invisible as faces on money. Easier to imagine the son than deal with how the father had turned out, the splotched, puffy flesh, lines incised in forehead and cheeks, strings dragging down the corners of the mouth. I switched off the light, let the merciful hood drop over the prisoner's head.

People don't really look, do they. Experiments have demonstrated conclusively how unobservant the average person is and, worse, how complacent, how unfazed by blindness. A man with a full beard gets paid to remove it and then goes about his usual day. The following day a researcher asks those who regularly encounter the man, his coworkers for example, if he had a beard when they saw him the previous day. Most can't remember one way or the other but assume he did. A few say the beard was missing. A few admit they'd never noticed a beard. A few insist vehemently they saw the invisible beard. I seem to recall the dead friend sporting a beard at one time or another during the period we were acquainted. Since I can't swear yes or no, I consign myself, just as Giacometti numbered himself, among the blind.

Are prisoners permitted to cultivate beards. Would a beard, if allowed, cause the son to resemble the father more closely. How would I recognize a resemblance if I can't visualize the father's face, or rather see it all too clearly as the anonymous blur of an aging man, any man, all men. Instead of staring without fear and taking responsibility for the unmistakable, beaten-up person I've apparently become, I prefer to see nothing.

Time at last for the visit. I'd written again and the son had responded again. A slightly longer reply with a visiting form tucked inside the flimsy prison envelope. Of course I couldn't help recalling the letter within a letter I'd received from the lawyer, Koppleman. The son instructed me to check the box for family and write *father* on the line following it. To cut red tape and speed up the process, I assumed, but for a second I hesitated, concerned some official would notice the names didn't match, then realized lots of inmates wouldn't bear (or know) their father's name, and some wouldn't claim it even though it's registered on their birth certificate, so I checked the family box, printed *father* in the space provided.

Aside from a few sentences *re* the enclosed form, the second letter actually shorter than the first: *Why not. My social calendar not full.* A smiling leopard in a cage. Step closer if you dare.

An official notice from the warden's office authorizing my visit took months to reach me. I began to regret lying on a form that had warned me, under penalty of law, not to perjure myself. Who reads the applications. How carefully did prison officials check facts applicants alleged. What punishments could be levied against a person who falsified information. The form a perfunctory measure, I guessed, so bureaucrats in charge of security could say they'd followed the rules. A form destined to gather dust in a file, properly executed and stamped, retrievable just in case an emergency exploded and some official needed to cover her or his ass. Justify his or her existence. The existence of the state. Of teeming prisons in the middle of the desert.

During the waiting my misgivings soured into mild paranoia. Had I compromised myself, broken a law that might send me too packing off to jail. I finally calmed down after I figured out that short of a DNA test (a) no one could prove I wasn't the prisoner's father and (b) it wasn't a crime to believe I was. If what the son had written in his first letter was true, the prison would possess no record of his father. The late friend past proclaiming his paternity. And even if he rose from the dead to argue his case, why would his claim, sans DNA confirmation, be more valid in the eyes of the law than mine. So what if he had visited. So what if he'd married the prisoner's mother. So what if he sincerely believed his belief of paternity. Mama's baby, Daddy's maybe. Hadn't I heard folks shout that taunt all my life. Didn't my own mother recite the refrain many times. Nasty

Kilroys scrawled everywhere on the crumbling walls of my old neighborhood hollered the same funny, mean threat. Careful, Jack. Don't turn your back. Kilroy's lurking. Kilroy's creeping. Keep your door locked, your ole lady pregnant in summer, barefoot in winter, my man. In more cases than people like to admit, paternity nothing but wishful thinking. Kilroy a thief in the night, leaves no fingerprints, no footprints. Mama's sweet baby, Daddy's, maybe.

Psychologists say there's a stage when a child doubts the adults raising it are its real family. How can parents prove otherwise. And why would kids want to trade in the glamorous fairy tales they dream up about their origins for a pair of ordinary, bumbling adults who impose stupid rules, stifling routines. Who needs their hostile world full of horrors and hate.

Some mornings when I awaken I look out my window and pretend to understand. I reside in a building in the bottom of somebody's pocket. Sunlight never touches its bricks. Any drawer or cabinet or closet shut tight for a day will exude a gust of moldy funk when you open it. The building's neither run-down nor cheap. Just dark, dank, and drab. Drab as grownups that children are browbeaten into accepting as their masters. The building, my seventh-floor apartment, languish in the shadow of something falling, leaning down, leaning over. Water, when you turn on a faucet first thing in the morning, gags on itself, spits, then gushes like a bloody jailbreak from the pipes. In a certain compartment of my heart where compassion's supposed to lodge, but there's never enough space in cramped urban dwellings so I store niggling self-pity there too, I try to find room also for all the millions of poor souls who have less than I have, who would howl for joy if they could occupy as their own one corner of my dreary little flat. I invite these unfortunates for a visit, pack the compartment till it's full far beyond capacity, and weep with them, share with them my scanty bit of prosperity, tell them I care, tell them be patient, tell them I'm on their side, tell them an old acquaintance of mine who happens to be a poet recently hit the lottery big-time, a cool million, and wish them similar luck, wish them clear sailing and swift, painless deaths, tell them it's good to be alive, whatever, tell them how much I appreciate living as long as I've managed and still eating every day, fucking now and then, finding a roof over my head in the morning after finding a bed to lie in at night, grateful to live on even though the pocket's deep and black and a hand may dig in any moment and crush me.

With Suh Jung's aid — why not use her, wasn't it always about finding uses for the people in your life, why would they be in your life if you had no use for them, or vice versa, and if you're using them, doesn't that lend purpose to their lives, you're actually doing them a trickle-down favor, aren't you, allowing them to use you to feel themselves useful and that's something, isn't it, better than nothing anyway, than being useless or used up — I gathered more information about the son in prison. Accumulated a file, biography, character sketch, rap sheet a.k.a. his criminal career.

You're going to wear out the words, she joked as she glanced over at me sitting beside her in the bed that occupied the same room with a Pullman fridge and stove. Her jibe less a joke than a complaint: I'm sick and tired of your obsessive poring over a few dog-eared scraps of paper extracted from Arizona's bottomless pit of records, is what she was saying with a slight curl of one side of her thin mouth, a grimace that could have been constructed as the beginning of a smirk she decided was not worth carrying full term.

I kept reading. Avoided the swift disappointment another glance at her tidy body would trigger. Its spareness had been exciting at first, but after the slow, slow, up-close-and-personal examination of her every square inch afforded by the bathing rituals she performed on me and I learned to reciprocate once my shyness abated, after we'd subjected each other's skin to washcloth, oil, the glide, pinch, stroke of fingertips and tongue, her body had become in a few months much less intriguing, less compensation for her tart remarks. Now I had no patience for her impatience with me, her taunts. The eroticism between us had dulled rather too quickly, it seemed. An older man's child-ish unreasonableness partly at fault. Why else would I be disap-pointed after a few weeks because her hips didn't round nor the negligible mounds beneath her nipples swell. Her boyish look not a stage, it was what I was going to get, period, even if the business between us survived longer than I had any reason to expect. No, things weren't going to get better, and I was wasting precious time. Given my age, how many more chances could I expect.

Here's what the papers said: He's done lots of bad things, the worst kinds of things, and if we could, we'd kill him, but we can't, so we'll never, never let him go.

Are you surprised, she'd asked.

I didn't know what to expect, I had replied.

Heavy-duty stuff. If only half the charges legit, he's a real bad actor.

I'm not traveling out West to forgive him or bust him out or bring him back. Just visit. Just fill in for the dead father. Once. One time enough and it's finished.

No matter how many times you read them, she says, the words won't change. Why read the same ugly facts over and over.

(A) Because my willing, skilled accomplice gathered them for me. (B) Curiosity.

His crimes would make a difference to me, I mean if I were you. This whole visiting business way over the top, you admit it yourself, so I don't pretend I can put myself in your shoes, but still. The awful crimes he's committed would affect anybody's decision to go or not.

Is he guilty. How can you be certain based on a few sheets of paper.

A lot's in the record. A bit too much for a case of mistaken identity. Huh-uh. Plus or minus a few felonies, the man's been busy.

Are you casting the first stone.

A whole building's been dumped on the poor guy. And he's thrown his share of bricks at other folks. I'd hate to bump into him in a dark alley.

Maybe you already have, my friend. Maybe you have and maybe you've enjoyed it.

You're more than a little weird about this, you know. What the hell are you talking about.

Just that people wind up in situations there's no accounting for. Situations when innocence or guilt are extremely beside the point. Situations when nothing's for sure except some of us are on one side of the bars, some on the other side, but nobody knows which side is which.

I know I haven't robbed or kidnapped or murdered anyone. Have you.

Have I. Do you really want to know. Everyone has crimes to answer for, don't they. Even you. Suppose I said my crimes are more terrible than his. Would you believe me. Would my confession start your heart beating a little faster.

(a) No. And (b) you're not scaring me. Put those damned papers away and turn off the light. Please. I have work tomorrow.

You don't want to hear my confession. It might sound better in the dark.

I'm tired. I need sleep, and you're acting stupid because you can't make up your mind to go to Arizona.

My mind's made up. The prison said yes. I'm on my way.

I'll be glad when it's over and done.

And me back in the arms of my love. Will you be faithful while your sweet serial killer's away.

She tries to snatch the papers but misses. I drop them over the side of the pull-out bed. Like the bed, she is small and light.

Easy to fold up and subdue even for an older fellow. When I wrap myself around her, my body's so much larger than hers, she almost vanishes. When we fuck, or now, capturing her, punishing her, I see very little of her flesh. I'm aware of my size, my strength towering over her squirming, her thrashing, her gasps for breath. I am her father's stare, the steel gate dropping over the tiger pit in which she's naked, trapped, begging for food and water. Air. Light.

I arrive on Sunday. Two days late, for reasons I can't explain to myself. I flew over mountains, then desert flatness that seemed to go on forever. It must have been Ohio, Illinois, Iowa, Nebraska, not actual desert but the nation's breadbasket, so they say, fruited plains, amber waves of grain, plowed, fertilized fields irrigated by giant machines day after day spreading water in the same pattern to create the circles, squares, rectangles below. Arable soil gradually giving way to sandy grit as the plane drones westward, through clouds, over another rugged seam of mountains, and then as I peer down at the undramatic nothingness beyond the far edge of wrinkled terrain, the surface of the earth flips over like a pancake. What's aboveground buried, what's belowground suddenly exposed. Upside-down mountains are hollow shells, deep, deep gouges in the stony waste, their invisible peaks underground, pointing to hell.

A bit of confusion, bureaucratic stuttering and sputtering when confronted by the unanticipated fact of my tardy arrival, a private calling his sergeant, sergeant phoning officer in charge of visitation, each searching for verification, for duplication, for assurance certified in black and white that she or he is off the hook, not guilty of disrupting the checks and balances of prison routine. I present myself hat in hand, remorseful, apologetic, *Please, please, give me another chance please kind sir,* forgive me for missing day one and two of the scheduled three-day visit, for checking in the morning of day three instead of day one. Am

I still eligible or will I be shooed away like starving beggars from the rich man's table.

I overhear two guards discussing a coyote whose scavenging brought it down out of the slightly elevated wilderness of rock and brush beginning a few miles or so from the prison's steel-fenced perimeter. I learn how patiently guards on duty in the tower spied on the coyote's cautious trespass of their turf, a blip at first, up and back along the horizon, then a discernible shape — skinny legs, long, pointed ears, bushy tail — a scraggly critter drawn by easy prey or coyote curiosity closer and closer to the prison until it was within rifle range and the guards took turns profiling it through their sharpshooting sniper scopes, the sad-faced, cartoon coyote they christened whatever guards would christen a creature they probably will kill one day, a spook, a mirage, it seems so quick on its feet, bolder as it's allowed to approach nearer without being challenged, believing perhaps it can't be seen, flitting from shadow to shadow, camouflaged by hovering darkness, by mottled fur, a shadow itself, instantly freezing, sniffing the air, then trotting again back and forth along the skyline, skittish through coverless space, up and back, parry, thrust, and retreat, ears pricked to attention when the rare service vehicle enters or leaves the prison parking lot before dawn. Murky predawn the coyote's time, the darkness divulging it, a drop from a leaky pipe, a phantom prowling nearer and nearer as if the electrified steel fence is one boundary of its cage, an easy shot now the sharpshooters forbear taking, too easy, or perhaps it's more fun to observe their mascot play, watch it pounce on a mouse and pummel it in swift paws bat-bat-bat before its jaws snap the rodent's neck or maybe the name they named it a kind of protection for a while till somebody comes on duty one morning or premorning really when the first shift after the night shift has to haul itself out of bed, out of prefab homes lining the road to the prison entrance, shitty box houses, a few with bright patches of something growing in flowerboxes beside the front steps, boxes you can't see at that black hour from your pickup, eyes locked in the tunnel your headlights carve, a bad-head, bad-attitude morning, pissed off, thinking about quitting this stinking job, getting the fuck out before you're caught Kilroying or cuckolded in the town's one swinging joint, cussed out, serving pussy probation till further notice, cancer eating his mama, daddy long gone, kids sick or fighting or crazy on pot or dead or in prison so he draws a bead and *pow,* blood seeps into the sand, the coyote buzzard bait by the time I eavesdrop on two guards badmouthing their assassin colleague, laughing at him, at the coyote's surprise, the dead animal still serving time as a conversation piece, recycled in this desert sparseness, desert of extremes, of keepers and kept, silence and screams, cold and hot, thirst and drunkenness, too much time, no time, where all's lost but nothing's gone.

A spiffy, spit-and-polish platinum blond guard whose nametag I read and promptly forget, Lieutenant, another guard addresses her, Lieutenant, each breast under her white blouse as large as Suh Jung's head, smiles up at me from the counter where she's installed, hands me the document she's stamped, slides me a tray for unloading everything in my pockets, stores it when I'm finished. Now that wasn't so bad, was it, sir. Gives me a receipt and a green ticket with matching numbers. Points me toward a metal detector standing stark and foursquare as a guillotine whose eye I must pass through before I'm allowed to enter the prison.

Beyond the detector one more locked door I must be buzzed through and I'm outside again, in an open-air, tunnel-like enclosure of Cyclone fencing bristling on sides and top with razor wire, a corridor or chute or funnel or maze I must negotiate while someone somewhere at a machine measures and records my every step, false move, hesitation, scream, counts drops of sweat, of blood when my hands tear at the razor wire, someone calibrating the before and after of my heart rate, my lungs.

I pass all the way through the tunnel to a last checkpoint, a small cinder-block hut squatting beside the final sliding gate guarding the visiting yard. Thirty yards away, across the yard, at a gated entranceway facing this one, guards are mustering inmates dressed in orange jumpsuits.

In a slot at the bottom of the hut's window you must surrender your numbered green ticket to receive a red one. Two groups of women and children ahead of me in line require a few minutes each for this procedure. Then I hold up the works. Feel on my back the helplessness and irritation of visits stalled. Five, ten minutes in the wire bullpen beside the hut, long enough to register a miraculous change in temperature. Less than an hour ago, crossing the parking lot from rental car to waiting room, I'd wondered if I'd dressed warmly enough for the visit. Now Arizona sun bakes my neck. I'm wishing for shade, for the sunglasses not permitted inside. My throat's parched. Will I be able to speak if spoken to. Through the hut's thick glass, bulletproof I'm guessing, I watch two officers chattering. One steps away to a wall phone. The other plops down at a shelflike minidesk, shuffles papers, punches buttons on a console. A dumb show since I couldn't hear a thing through the slab of greenish glass.

Did I stand in the cage five minutes or ten or twenty. What I recall is mounting heat, sweat rolling inside my clothes, blinking, losing track of time, not caring about time, shakiness, numbness, mumbling to myself, stiffening rage, morphing combinations of all the above, yet overriding each sensation, the urge to flee, to be elsewhere, anywhere other than stalled at that gate, waiting to be snatched inside or driven away or, worse, pinned there forever. Would I be knocked down to my knees, forced to recite my sins, the son's sins, the sins of the world. If I tried to escape, would my body—*splat*—be splashed and pulped on the razor wire or could I glide magically through the knives glinting like mirrors, not stopping till I reach a spot far, far away where I can bury my throbbing head in the coolness miles deep below the sand, so deep you can hear the subterranean chortle of rivers on the opposite face of the planet.

At last someone arrives from a door I hadn't noticed, addressing me, I think.

Sorry. Your visit's been canceled. Computer says the inmate you want to visit is not in the facility. Call the warden's office after 9 A.M. Monday. Maybe they can give you more information. Sorry about the mix-up. Now please stand back. Step away from the gate so the next . . .

Fanon

"Today I believe in the possibility of love."

— Frantz Fanon

I.

ON THE SCREEN they are chopping up Lumumba and burning his body parts in an oil drum. Two thick, red-faced, unhappy louts. Brueghel peasants sweating through khaki uniforms, working overtime to clean up the Belgian king's mess. I imagine Chantal beside me, imagine us going to a bar after the movie, and maybe I'll attempt to explain my reaction when I was a kid and first heard Lumumba's name. His name and the others — Kasavubu, Mobutu, Tshombe. Names embarrassing me, sounding like tom-toms, like jibber-jabber blabbered through big African lips at Tarzan or bwana in Hollywood movies. Black, sweaty native faces. Fat eyes rolling and showing too much white. Would I tell her I'd heard my white friends giggling at the funny names even as the news reported rape, massacres, chaos in faraway countries. Terrified Europeans fleeing, wild Africans seizing power. Mumbo-jumbo names. Cannibal names. Nigger names coming to get me. Lumumba-Tshombe-Mobutu-Kasavubu.

In Accra, Ghana, in 1960, Frantz Fanon met Patrice Lumumba. Both spoke French, Chantal's language, both were thirty-five, and in the next year both would die, Lumumba murdered in the Congo at the beginning of 1961, Fanon succumbing to leukemia in the U.S.A. at the year's end.

Today I'm much older than these dead men lived to be, these fallen heroes once old enough to be my fathers. Now I am old enough to have a son of thirty-five. How could so many years be lost in an instant. Everything and nothing changing. When Lumumba and Fanon died, I was a boy setting out to conquer the world, a world that, by disposing of them, had expressed its scorn, its determination to prevent boys like me from conquering much of anything. Mercifully or unmercifully, I knew next to nothing about either man back in 1961; I was full of myself, studying hard to win a college scholarship, intoxicated by what I believed were infinite possibilities, unlimited time. Now I understand (and believe me, derive no satisfaction from the fact) that my ignorance of these men, of their countries and legacy, did not indicate simply a personal failure of imagination. Particular kinds of information and knowledge had been erased by my education. Erased ruthlessly, systematically, with malice, just as Patrice Lumumba, Frantz Fanon, and countless others — perhaps our best women and men — have been struck down and erased.

Neither Chantal nor I recognized the face stenciled with black spray paint on a greenish gray metal shed whose purpose we didn't recognize either in a field we passed each day on our walks back and forth to the beach. Though we remained slightly curious about this somehow familiar face staring back at us, the face and the Arabic script beneath were small details during the three weeks we spent on Martinique over a Christmas holiday a dozen years ago. We were too busy falling in love. Busy fucking our brains out, so to speak. The island a perfect third partner, nibbling, provoking, overloading our senses, enslaving us subtly as we became accustomed to the constant attention of sun, palm trees sighing, the surf's murmur, the breeze's caressing fingers. But once it had registered, the face, like the island's enchanting complicity, never entirely disappeared.

Strangely, the hotel staff, other guests, shopkeepers, couldn't name the face, and most claimed to be unaware of its existence in the field where a few pale long-horned cattle were tethered near the road's edge to graze. Could the face be one of the island's fabled ghosts, a revenant, playing us. If we stopped believing, if we blinked, would it go away.

One afternoon a young man on a bicycle, an island native whose small round head bristled with spiky braids, happened to be pedaling toward us, idly zigzagging from one edge of the road to the other, and reached us just as we were opposite the shed. In English, French, and sign language we hailed him, and Chantal asked about the face. Straddling his undersized bike, supporting its weight with one foot on the ground, he stared at the shed, as if surprised it had sprouted in the field since his last trip up the road. Then he firmly shook his head, no, no, turning over his brown hands to prove they too were innocent.

A big smile said he wished to be helpful, but he shrugged his bare, bony shoulders after a glance at the shed. Now his turn to be curious, checking out Chantal, meeting my gaze for the first time before quickly hiding his eyes behind long, curled lashes. I could hear his thoughts. Whoever else I'd become, wouldn't I always be a shy, skinny brown kid daydreaming on a bike. Who are these strangers worried about a face painted on the side of a metal box, a beat-up face and gang tags and scribble-scrabble writing. Why are these people minding my business, stopping me, bothering me about a face nobody sees, this pretty blond woman and a man as brown as me with nothing better to do than stroll half naked, white hand in black hand, like trouble itself, up and down my road, on my island, asking questions about stuff nobody with good sense cares about, not asking my name, not offering some little work and tip, why else they think I be pedaling the live-long day up and back, up and back, scuffling for a little change.

When we reached the entrance to the beach, I looked back

over my shoulder. The boy hadn't moved from the spot where we'd left him, the minibike, his long, lean body sidesaddle astride it printed hazily against the glare, a Giacometti stick figure frozen yet moving, watching the field sleep.

Fanon didn't claim the crude, spray-painted replica of his face until I recalled he'd been born there, on the French island of Martinique, and once that connection had reconnected in my brain, other memories were freed—his face in a photo snapped during the first *Presence africaine* conference in Paris in the fifties, his face on the back cover of *The Wretched of the Earth*, a color shot of him illustrating a magazine review of *Black Skin, White Mask*. Of course it's Frantz Fanon. Who else. Why had it taken me so long to recognize him. To recognize the sadness and anger of his gaze. His eyes staring through me. Who are you. Why are you here on my island with this woman. Is it so easy to become one of them.

On the rooftop of my apartment building one morning last fall, the draft of my Fanon book open, waiting for me to begin again, I was distracted by an enormous plume of dark smoke billowing above the skyline. A constant scream and hoot and whine of sirens in the streets below. Before long tenants who'd been watching TV began to gather on the roof, and from their stunned, disbelieving comments I learned that planes had rammed the Twin Towers and the giant buildings were burning.

Just the day before, in an oddly begrudging, ambivalent biography of Frantz Fanon written by a guy who seemed basically to mistrust and underestimate Fanon's intelligence even as he painstakingly constructed a monumental life for his subject, I had read that Fanon defined the Third World as a *colossal mass* facing Europe and that the Third World's *project* must be to resolve problems to which Europe has found no solutions. The face stenciled on the wall was speaking again: Someone's tired of waiting for Europe. The project has begun.

◆ ◆ ◆

According to the dreadlocked brother waiting tables at Aunt Kizzy's snack stand, this road should take us to the best beaches. I'm losing faith as the road narrows, roughens, ain't hardly road no more, an obstacle course of steep ruts, hulking boulders, potholes, a mud-colored track between margins definitely not road, to my left reedy muck that could swallow the tiny rental car without a burp, to my right squatty trees whose gray roots and branches braid into an impenetrable tangle running low along the ground. Glimpses of ocean pop into view, the promised land drawing me on. I dodge rocks, drop blindly over precipices where there might or might not be more road for the tires to grab.

After a steep climb, we shed a rocky wall blocking our view and below us, at the foot of an immense seam of stone, sea sparkles, visible to the horizon. I slow the car to take in the view. Just beyond a jumble of boulders edging a stone shelf that's pocked and furrowed like an ancient face, yes, yes, golden sand stretches. A few bodies are visible sunning on exposed ledges or hunkered in caves of stone, but the beach appears empty as paradise.

Blacktop now, the road descends as abruptly as it rose, continues on level ground. Woods conceal the water until we reach a line of tall trees straight and bare as fenceposts. Through rows of black trunks we can cop peeks of crackling ocean, sand bleached nearly white just before it meets turquoise water.

This is what we've been looking for. Hungry for. Remember how quickly we unpacked the car. You never looked more gorgeous, girl. Your orange sarong transparent as orange tissue paper as you *chaloupe* in and out of shafts of light spilling through a roof of leaves and branches. Returning to the day now, I don't need to invent to make it perfect. Blue sky, hot sun, whitecaps breaking on miles of gloriously vacant beach.

Forgive the guidebook tone. Your memory for detail better than mine anyway. This map I'm drawing more for me than you. Stopping time on this page so the island can't change.

We swam naked. Or rather, you swam and I played in water up to my chest, performing my clumsy riff on body surfing, wishing I hadn't grown up in a city with segregated pools, wishing I'd learned to be a fish like you. When you shoot out of the water next to me, grinning from ear to ear, you look so fine I have to scoop you into my arms. Your hair's plastered like dreadlocks to your skull, bright beads of water stick to your lashes, pearls on the tips of your ears. Then you slide down my chest into the water and while I grip your hands you float on your back, a spoke in a turning wheel, till you kick back into my arms and I lift you again. Breakers smack our backs, splash our faces. The water's roar drowns whatever silliness we holler back and forth. I'm pulled deeper by the current, a step too deep, and a wave punches my feet out from under me. I lose my grip on you and you stroke into a high foaming wall of water, last thing I see until I pop up and regain my footing, spitting, coughing, arms flailing like I'm beating out a fire.

Later that afternoon company arrived. A few strollers up and down the beach. Some clothed, some not. So it was demiparadise, roll your own rules. No need to cover up, you decided. Nothing to hide from strangers a city block away, meandering along the water's edge. Then a tall guy tanned black as a native settles down maybe twenty yards away, spreading out his towel nonchalantly, pretending to ignore us but really — I spy on him as intently as he spies on you — he can't take his eyes off you. Belly-flopped on the hot sand, peering over the top of my book, I try to guard you and let you go, pretending the man's eyes can't hurt you, can't spoil our privacy.

I hoped I could slay my demons that day by watching another man's eyes on you, a white man no less. Believed I might free myself of jealousy that day and maybe in the days to come if

I stayed clear about what could or couldn't be stolen from us, what couldn't be owned or possessed.

I was mistaken. Even before the shouting match next morning, I had been squirming all night watching you in other men's arms. Black men, white men, doing whatever they pleased with your body. You offered them the same eyes, same lips and smiles you offered me. I woke up angry, drenched in sweat. Aroused and ashamed. Hungry for you. Afraid to touch you. I hated myself for making you up, making up the island. Scrubbing it clean of shadows. Playing hide-and-seek with Fanon's face. Stealing an island that belonged to its African dead. Who will never own it, never leave. Their screams, bones, and blood the island's flesh.

One of those thirty-minute downpours kept us in bed the last morning on Martinique. While the weather cleared, we drank coffee and talked. At first light I'd gone outside to the little covered terrace, tried to ignore the bad dreams, calm myself with the ritual of fixing our coffee on the propane stove. Back beside you, waiting for you to waken, I'd listened to the silence of the sky darkening, then to the palm trees rustling and rattle. Do you remember how they imitate the sound of rain pounding long before the rain starts, then the same sound again after rain's over.

The white guy staring at you on the beach yesterday. What do you think he was thinking.

Nothing much. Men, black or white, believe it's their duty to stare at women.

His stare white not black. The master checking out his property.

Black or white. Why is there always a difference for you. The man on the beach could have been gay, peeping at you maybe. Or black and white. Black or white makes no difference to me. I have probably been with more black men than white. To my eyes black men, they . . . you are more beautiful, more fun usually.

Forbidden fun.

Yes and no. Plenty of French people do not like to see black with white. But not like in America. Not your terrible lynching.

Black or white doesn't matter in Paris, right. Except black more beautiful, huh. Plenty of handsome Africans and West Indians to pick from. Why bother with white fellas. Why fuck that Antoine.

Why are you speaking in such an ugly way. Years since I've seen Antoine. Why are you talking about him. I love you.

You're not being honest with me. Or yourself. You say you've known him ten years. C'mon. That ain't no casual affair. Your Great White Hope, you just don't want to admit it.

Stop it. I've known him a long time, yes. But no way we were lovers that long. Never really lovers. Not love like we have. For years at a time I might not see him.

Except when he called, you'd go. Right. And fuck him again, right.

You're not listening. I've told you many times that was a small part of it.

But it always happened, didn't it. Must have been some kind of special attraction. Why would you keep going back, if not. His whiteness maybe. A change of pace from your fun black boys. A little white-French-boy homecoming for you.

Don't be an idiot. If he was passing through the city and I had no attachments, why not see him. I never said I didn't enjoy his company. If I was free when he called, we'd get together. It happened a few times over the years. I never wanted more. Believe me, I could have made it more. I'm sure he liked me, but I knew better than to fall in love with a man like him. He was terrible with women.

Okay. Maybe you were smart enough not to fall in love. But you weren't willing to give up on him, either. You left the door open. Let him use you.

We used each other. He needed help on a project in the Caribbean. It was winter. I was between jobs. Broke. Depressed.

New York can be so gray and horrible in February. He offered me work. A week on a tropical island. Why would I say no.

More than a job, wasn't it. You both understood quite well he was offering more than a job.

He was my friend. A man who could make me laugh. Of course I said yes.

If a condition of the bargain is fucking him, isn't that more than friendship.

Is it. No one forced me to do anything. I chose to go. Enjoyed the trip. I needed to be away from the city. From my troubles. Needed someone to look after me, make me feel alive, feel like a woman.

I guess he did just that, huh. Made you feel like a woman.

Not the way I feel with you. Not the way I feel with you on our island, my love. Please stop. A different time, a different place. Not our island.

Different, you say. Another island, you say. Different time. Different place. Fuck that. It's always the same goddamn island.

Dear Chantal,

It's raining this morning, and I hear your voice teaching me Verlaine. Il pleut dans la ville. Il pleut dans mon coeur. Stumbling out of bed last night to pee, I stubbed my toe. Cursed myself. Cursed the inventor of wine. No need to check the clock. Every night my 3 A.M. terrorist slaps me awake. Tortures confessions from me. Some nights I never get back to sleep. With so much misery and murder everywhere, why should anybody sleep soundly. The clock's ticking. Time's running out. The 3 A.M. wake-up call reminds me I'm not exempt. I can't be black and white, rich and poor, guilty and innocent. Ain't never been rich but you know what I mean, jellybean. Ashes, ashes, we're all falling down.

But I'm not writing to fuss about the state of the world. I'm writing to say hello. How are you? Where are you? We've lost touch so I can't mail this epistle, but I'm going to bundle myself up in it and walk the streets like one of those sandwich-board people. Perhaps a kind stranger will read the words and pass them on to another stranger and so forth till one day a stranger passes them on to you. Wouldn't that be something. Would it be enough to bring you back from the dead. Summon me from the dead. Where, oh where has my sweet lamb strayed.

II.

She's alone, sitting up in bed watching dawn ignite the window blind's edges, arms hugging her drawn-up knees, remembering how quiet Paul became the last morning on Martinique. Quiet after shouting accusations, after bruising her shoulders, after making love. No more questions about other men. He'd become one of them, his features blurring, dissolving, any man, no man. She remembers his empty, unfocused smile when, finally, he got up from her side and stood naked at the bathroom door. Remembers herself naked too, sitting up like this, wondering who he saw. Wonders, would he be jealous today if she told him she's fallen in love with Osama bin Laden's sad eyes.

Somewhere Paul sits fussing with the Fanon book he'll never finish. She wishes this certainty could comfort her on a gray morning, chill air misting the suddenly vulnerable windows on the top floor of her high-rise, the wind's moaning and groaning, amplified as it swirls around balconies, gusts into corners, shrieks from ground to roof in air shafts. A gigantic thud buckles the building. She wipes the glass, expects to see bricks toppling, falling in rows precise as formations of geese, but instead, needles of rain slant, invisible unless she stares and stares . . .

Paul's somewhere poring over yellow sheets of tablet paper. Cramped, scrawled words written, unwritten, rewritten, layers of words too thickly impacted for anyone not Paul to decode.

Will he ever decipher them. Could he if he tried. Hunched over a desk or slumped in a cushioned armchair, a mug of sludgy black coffee near at hand. How many mornings had she awakened to the scene. Fascinating at first. Yes. Reassuring. Whether she wakes up or not, he'll be there. Steadfast. Undistractable. His reliability more than a routine. His nature. Who he is. She can count on it. Him worrying the manuscript no matter what else is going on in the world. Then the steadiness begins to grate. Some mornings she wants to hit him. Blurt out, *How dare you*. Worse than all that, finally, was getting used to him, sorry for him once she understood he had no choice.

Why does she still depend on that vexed certainty. Wishing for his company no matter how negative, how abstract. Why does she need him out there, no matter where she finds herself, rain-soaked morning or dry. Out there so she can ignore him or argue with him or root for him or miss him as she does this morning, missing him, wanting to grab him by the scruff of the neck, rattle his bones, shake him out of his dream. You're missing it, man. Missing and missed.

I can only write the present, he claimed, because the past is too complicated. I remember the past too well. The present's easy to forget. Nobody remembers it, nobody believes it, so the present's easy to forge, easy to turn into fiction.

She recalls the notion of negative dependability from some literary pundit's discussion of narrative. How certain characters couldn't help themselves. They lied because they knew no other way. Lied even when the truth obviously would serve them better. Always twisting or exaggerating the facts or flat-out making up shit to suit their purposes, their only purpose – to lie. Do these liars offer a ray of hope in an undependable world. If you precisely discounted what the American president said, scrupulously deflated or inflated or reversed or ignored or denied, could you approximate truth. Reliably estimate at least what wasn't so. Is that why Paul declared his Fanon book must be fiction. Is it why she reads romances voraciously, giggling at her dopey gullibility while she turns pages and weeps. If she subtracts the lies she wishes to believe and adds untruths liars tell, can she calculate the truth of her life, the truth of this dying city through whose wet, heavy air she sends Paul a greeting this morning, wishing it were a song, wishing he'd hear her voice, jump up and dance.

She can name the day and month but can't recall where they last spoke face to face. A bench in Central Park. A sidewalk café on the Lower East Side. Sitting outdoors. Somewhere public. Safe, neutral ground. Why had they grown so afraid of each other. Afraid of being alone together in the dark.

I miss you

I miss you

It's better this way, I think

Who says so

I should have listened the last morning on Martinique. You told me you could never forgive me. You were telling the truth. You'll always blame me for the past, for things that happened before we met.

I was in love. Confused because I was hopelessly in love.

We both were. And love made both of us insanely jealous. Me more than you, probably, though you were the one who used your jealousy as a weapon. Questioning me. Pushing till I said too much or too little. Until something broke. I never had a chance to speak of my own fears. I would picture you naked with a woman. Your hands in her hair. Touching her. Her looking at your body. Sometimes I'd want to scream. Those images could shatter my confidence. Who was I. The newness would wear off and you'd look somewhere else for newness. And then it happened. We hadn't been back here a month before you fucked another woman. So much for love. So much for our island.

A dumb thing to do. Dumb. Dumb. No excuse. I still don't

understand why it happened. Not the woman. Only once. No desire to see her ever again.

You used her to punish me. She was payback. As if I owed you something for the men in my past. As if it was your turn to hurt me. You had warned me in Martinique. My fault I didn't listen.

You wouldn't talk to me. Why did you keep everything inside.

Talk. What could I say. Should I have talked the way you talked to me. *White bitch.* Waking me up in the middle of the night. *White whore.* Refusing to look at me. Touch me.

I loved you and it scared me. I needed to understand everything about you. I needed you to help me understand.

Fanon's face on the shed. Remember.

What's his face got to do with it.

You needed him more than you needed me.

Whoa. Who said I didn't need you. You're the one who flew away to Paris.

I came back.

I'm still not clear why. Or why you split.

You left me no choice. Maybe when we saw Fanon painted on the wall, it was already too late. I should have listened. Fanon speaking from the grave.

The last morning on Martinique plays again, the rainy window a screen.

I want to hear the whole story this time. So tell me again. About you and him that night on the island.

We shouldn't have been there. I knew it, even before I heard a man following us through the street.

Yes. She'd known it that night on the island with Antoine. Knew it in the deep place where things people don't want to know are known. The knowledge of things that sooner or later will hurt you or kill you because you pretend they're not there.

They'd stayed in the newspaper office too late. Their color all wrong when they stepped from the building into the dark streets, all wrong and begging for trouble in a back-of-the-wall ghetto, barrio, slum, estimate, medina, favela. She'd learned lots of words for the entrapping evil and saying none of them helped. *Merde . . . plus vite, marche, Chantal . . . marche plus vite.* She'd caught panic in Antoine's eyes, a split second of naked pleading when he thought she couldn't see his face.

Wrong and stupid. I know, Paul.

Very stupid. Night or day.

Yes, you're right.

So what happened.

Well, nothing happened, really. We were stupid but lucky, I guess. I'm positive somebody followed us. Footsteps behind us clack-clack-clacking in a long narrow street with walls almost up to the curbs. You feel you've blundered inside someone's house. Totally deserted ahead and neither of us dared turn around, but out of the corner of my eye I saw movement, a shadow maybe, maybe my own shadow. Whatever, it was enough to make me sure the man stalking us was about to catch up. We were in a place we shouldn't be. He'd found us and we belonged to him.

He's always there. You sense it in your bones, whether or not you see or hear him. In certain parts of town, after dark your color makes you guilty. You're scared when footsteps start clack-clack-clacking behind you, clack-clack on the cobble-stones, almost matching yours but a little before or after. Footsteps playing with your head the way one of those smiling African smoothies in a club gets you out on the dance floor and you can't keep up, it's his music, he's in charge.

Bet you weren't thinking about dancing in the dark, sweetheart.

No. I was frightened. Very frightened. And furious at myself because I'd lost my chance to speak. What could I say if he pulled out a gun or knife. *Please don't hurt poor, innocent me.*

So there you were. White woman with a white man in the blackest, poorest, most dangerous section of one of the most dangerous black cities anywhere on earth and you weren't thinking about dancing, right, you were scared shitless and this big-deal, big-guy buddy or boss or lover or fellow fool, whatever, he's shaking in his booties too. What I want to know is not so much why. People usually have reasons, lamebrained or otherwise, for what they do, so I assume your reasons probably made sense to you at the time — a deadline maybe for your project and pushing to finish or maybe the work fascinating and you lose track of the hour or maybe you'd been on the island long enough to start feeling comfortable everybody nice to you showing you around hanging out at night in the clubs with the locals smoking ganja with Rasta brothers in the hills feeling you're loved here in spite of centuries of white crimes against black people the daily misery and humiliation of arriving at the threshold of the twenty-first century and still being starved robbed beaten in what's spozed to be your own country still a boy or a wench still bending over and taking it up the ass for tips tourists toss at you maybe you believed you'd transcended that boring old-school colonized and colonizer oppressed and oppressor bullshit and could start fresh a new world order and everybody just people after all, all colors shapes sizes smells but just plain folks after all. Shit. Or maybe you and your white fella finished work in the office he'd rented for his project and got horny thinking about pretty, naked brown flesh surrounding you every day on the island, the island lilt of voices, how hips sway and shoulders dip and butts pout, flimsy native costumes more come-on than cover-up, to say nothing of the drums, the singing and dancing, the sunshine and sparkling sea pumping you up so you turn off your cell phones, pack away your papers and computers, lock the office door, and get it on, the whole sweaty, heavy-breathing nasty atop a desk, spiced by images of handsome natives brushing past you on the busy streets, brown muscles brown dicks and titties brown funk and bushy hair. Maybe a sudden irresistible pussy call kept you late at the office but like I said before the reason's not what really interests me. I want to know what you imagined. Who you believed you were. Two white Europeans parading after dark through the grungiest, most unforgiving, most violent, blackest quarter of the town. The two of you well fed, tanned, pretty, *Beg pardon folks, just passing through,* through the cesspool your bad intentions and good intentions created, the sewage in which human beings must make lives for themselves swimming in centuries of your filth. What did you imagine yourselves doing. What do you imagine you're doing with me. What gives you the right to rub the privilege of your whiteness, your immunity, in dying people's faces. Slinking through a place so down and out even niggers with nothing to lose avoid it if they can. Dog-eat-dog back-of-the-wall and at night too. Who the fuck did you think you were. What kind of daydream were you strolling around in.

She survived it. That's all she can say for sure. Or wishes to say to herself. Survived the stupid, trespassing night. Survived Paul's angry words years after the night. Survived his betrayal, the breakup, the end of their time together. Survived their trip to the island Paul could not keep separate from other trips, other islands, other men. Survived Paul's hands on her, hurting her shoulders the last morning on Martinique. His screaming, crying. Hers. Survived in a fashion, she's quick to add, reminding herself or whomever she's speaking to this rainy morning that surviving covers lots of ground, that survival may be everything and it's also nothing. Checks herself, wonders if she really means that, checks the eyes of the one she's addressing, it could be Paul, him here next to her quietly listening, eyes filling up with tears as he follows where she leads, into the abyss, the chances they'd squandered, the scorched earth, his scorched fingers digging into her scorched flesh, wanting to hurt, to rip, shaking her till she submits, her head flopping side to side as he looms above her, shaking, shaking, shaking whiteness out and blackness in or blackness out and whiteness in, she remembers thinking some crazy true thought like that just before she stopped caring and let her body sink and die.

III.

They say that toward the end of her life, or you could say when her life was over, the cops gathered what was left of Marilyn Monroe after she'd finally binged enough booze and pills to kill herself and rushed her body to Bellevue or some other mental ward, where she was stripped and deposited in a padded, brightly lit rubber room. Throughout the night, as word of her presence spread, a steady trickle of cops and hospital personnel arrived to take turns peering through the peephole of the cubicle where Marilyn Monroe lay on display naked, sleeping her drugged last sleep.

I think of poor Marilyn Monroe when I try to visualize Frantz Fanon's final days in a Bethesda, Maryland, hospital room, curious doctors, nurses, interns trooping in and out to observe him, this Fanon they'd heard awful things about, a fiery, white-hating black revolutionary, prophet of terror, now helpless, dazed, unable to speak, dying of leukemia, a disease characterized by an overload of leucocytes, white corpuscles in the blood that suppress other cells. Fanon seized by fits of vomiting and diarrhea as he fights to rid his system of poison, poison causing hyperpigmentation, Fanon's skin blacker and blacker, like Patrice Lumumba's skin when his body parts cooked in a rusty oil barrel. Fanon and Marilyn chained together, stuffed in the hold of a slave ship crossing the Atlantic. Naked, shitting, pissing, throwing up on each other as the creaking wooden vessel's tossed by stormy seas. Then during a calm they are hauled on deck to dance. What should we name the dance they perform under the eyes of the crew, the dance timed by a crackling cat-o'-nine-tails a drunken sailor snaps at their bare, filthy, bloody, beautiful backs.

Hello. My name is Marilyn.

Hi. I'm Frantz.

Haven't we met before.

It could have happened.

Hard to be sure, isn't it. It's so dark below. And so dazzling up here. I have to squint to see you. How can they keep staring at us without going blind.

Perhaps they are blind. Perhaps we are too.

Here, take my hand, Frantz.

Take my temperature, my blood pressure, my pulse.

Why are they doing this. Why can't they take their eyes off us. What do they expect to see.

I'm very sick. I arrived in this country sick and they put something in my food every day to make me sicker. I'm worried I won't survive to finish my book.

Don't worry. You'll finish. And I promise to read every word.

Thank you, miss.

Oh, Frantz. I'm so cold. Hold me. Never let me go. Maybe we won't die. Maybe there's hope.

I never thought you . . . I never thought we would end up like this.

It doesn't end like this. This is just a dream. We're trapped in someone's evil dreaming. Sleep, sleep, my pumpkin. Soon we'll wake up in another dream. Everything will be different . . .

> *Happy birthday to you*
> *Happy birthday to you*
> *Happy birthday, dear Frantz,*
> *Happy birthday to you.*

Who Weeps When One of Us
Goes Down Blues

WHEN ARCHIE SATTERWHITE went down, you could hear it all over the arena, from courtside reserved to the corporate boxes to the cheap seats in heaven, the dull thud of Archie's back slamming the hardwood floor. Did his skull strike first. Did we censor the sharp crack of bone. Is Archie ever going to stir or speak. We've formed a circle. We've done it before, so the circle's wide, with plenty of room for trainer, coach, and Archie in the center, for a doctor if one's in the house. Breathing space for the fallen one. For us. Though none of us seems to breathe for a while. Every player in the circle as still as Archie's dark, long body stretched on the arena floor. Damn, Archie. You got some big feet, man. Look at that boy's size nine-teens sticking up in the air. Be eight foot tall if so much of him wasn't turned under. You think dumb stuff like that when somebody goes down hard, bad hard, and no thought fits, just like no look feels right on your face. Some guys smirk. Some freeze their features into impenetrable masks. Some wag their heads as if in conversation with another innocent bystander shocked by a sudden, brutal accident. Some faces are happy: I told you so, didn't I, their faces say. Didn't I tell you so. And there are the stunned, the glaze-eyed, the painfully concerned or unconcerned. Some can't hide their impatience. Blame the fallen one for disrupting the flow. Some guys turn their backs and stroll to the bench. Some bow their heads to conceal their reaction. Me, I'll study the rafters, pan the other players' faces. Staring at the dome's ceiling, I wear a look of detachment, resignation. I've heard the verdict, await the sentence. Or, since any face serves as well as any other, I check out my teammates, let one be my guide.

All of us understand it's just a matter of time. Sooner or later, in one way or another, everybody goes down. Each player extends a little unspoken blip of gratitude toward the one whose time to fall has come, thanks him for taking a turn so it's not anybody else's turn. Since the truth is somebody's always falling and the other truth is it's got to be one of us, deep down we admit to ourselves, Better him than me. The final truth—we're glad it's him. Other emotions primped up on our faces are mostly bullshit to cover up what's in the gut pit where the real deal lives.

I drop my eyes from the mile-high, exposed steel underwear of this domed, multisport, mega-event palace and mirror the face on the tallest head, the head belonging to Norman Oakes, our gentle big man. Remember the Jolly Green Giant in the frozen vegetable ads. Well, Norman Oakes's not bright green like him, but he's huge, goofy-looking, deep-voiced, and comical like the Giant. Norman no color really, he goes from pale as a ghost to pinkish to red to a gray dingy as bedsheets in crummy hotels where they used to stick us my first seasons in the league. Not white, not broccoli green, no permanent shade, even though he tries his best to go for black.

Norman's all flustered by a shit-eating grin he can't wipe off his big mug. Seven-foot-two and probably still growing, a soft, dumb-ox, flummoxy, country-looking white boy who can't hold back the grin anybody with half a brain and a smidgen of common sense would know better than to be grinning at a time like this.

He dresses in black. With lots of metal, lots of tattoos. They call it Gothic. To me it's plain ole Nazi. Owns the biggest carcass in the league but wilts (no disrespect to you, Mr. Chamberlain, the old original Goliath) if a black player of any size or color barks at him. Now, we got some large, surly, charcoal-broiled black brothers in this league and a few of these hard-legs put the fear of God in anybody, including yours truly, but plenty light-in-the-ass, light-complected, roadrunner-type black dudes too. Guess our Norman's like an elephant. Large as your average elephant grows, it still gets squirmy, worrying about little creatures scurrying and scampering in and out of the shadows at its feet. Or maybe since he's so blond and pale, Norman believes people can look right through his skin, figures maybe they see his sneaky mean streak, his evil thoughts, see through tons of pink meat and peep the hole card of his scaredy-cat heart.

Anyway, on the night Archie doesn't make it off the floor till they slide him onto a gurney, crank it up, and roll my man out the swinging doors, I take a cue from Norman's uncolored face looming half a head higher than just about everybody else's in the circle. With Archie laid out and still ain't twitched a muscle and the awful thought cruising our minds that he might not ever move except in a wheelchair, Norman's face does its best imitation of very serious, very unsuccessfully cause he can't hide the fact he's about to crack up. Something tickling the fool, no doubt about it. You know, like a big, scrubbed boy in the vestibule of a church, surrounded by his little-bitty mom and a posse of proper blue-haired old biddies and he's trying to act all nice while inside his balloon head he's jerking off or giggling at some nasty joke. Norman's lips quiver, he sucks in his peach-fuzzed cheeks, shyly lowers his gaze, covers his mouth with a ham-sized hand. None of it's working. Any second the clown will bust out laughing.

I chose Norman Oakes's face. Call up a wild story with no business being here, something dumb and raunchy I should be ashamed of thinking at a time like this, dissing Archie's danger, dissing myself and the rest of the players around me who make faces, make believe they know which face fits when one of us goes down and the game stops and may be over for good for the one down.

Why not. Any look right as anyone else's. I don't pick it exactly. It picks me. Like the blues picks me certain days. A look on my face to get me through the blank space till play resumes. Because the game always resumes, doesn't it. We count on it. Isn't that why we bop till we drop.

Bopping till you drop's what they pay you for when you play major league for major bucks. Always on the road. One city fades into the next and you stop asking Where we headed next cause you're already there. But hey, fans think major leaguers got a lot going for themselves. And in a way we do. Money, yeah, and youth for a minute, talent, a small bit of fame, or publicity at least, enough so people are aware, some people anyway, aware when we hit town, aware we bring money to burn, exotic ways, quick hands, lean muscles, our burning, restless eyes. Why wouldn't city after city spread its legs for us. Here today, gone tomorrow. It's what being on the road means. The city opens doors never open for nobody not on the road. Doors marked *Black git back.* Doors so the city can sneak out and act a fool. Get juke-joint happy. Hucklebuck, drink moonshine, tell lies, and crawl up under our large, sweaty bodies. Like those old down-home tunes people hear a thousand times, just got to hear one more once again, we are welcome as a known quantity and as a mystery. An unbeatable combination whether the home team kicks our ass or we kick theirs.

People pay good money to watch us. Love us because we prove they are not alone. Maybe the game's main attraction. For fans. For us. Proving we are not alone. Proving the city's real. Must be a city outside the arena. Where else would the crowd come from. Where else would fans return after a game. Has to be a city to house all the unlucky people too poor to buy tickets.

Fans read scores, catch highlights on TV of games played in faraway cities. We prove a whole, big, fabulous country's out there, stretching from coast to coast, its cities glittering beads we string together, a country pitch dark until our long fingers hit a light switch and everything's bright and comfy as a suite in a high-class hotel.

Even if you're home alone, checking out a game on the tube, you're safe and connected like people on those cell phones every man, woman, and baby got to have nowadays to show there's somebody somewhere takes their calls, and shit it might be Michael Jordan or Ms. Universe on the other end of the line for all you know, sucker, their faces say when you pass people talking to themselves on the street.

Depending on the hour of our flight, a city slides into view peekaboo through layers of clouds and smog or it swims in blackness ten million quilts of light can't cover. On the ground we're shuttle-bused from airport to hotel to playing site, the city a maze of expressways, boulevards, avenues, streets with familiar names, same names we've read elsewhere on signs drivers followed to wind up in the same place these different signs with the same names will lead us tonight. Here we go again, time to go to work again. We learn to nap and drowse our way through cities, their presence faint as however many ticks of our Rolexes, however many ticks of our hearts required to count down the space separating us from the moment a referee blows a whistle and summons both teams for the tip-off at center court. Once I woke up sitting half naked on a bench in front of an open locker and no clue whether I should be putting on clothes or taking them off.

Some nights you hope the game will last forever. Or wish it had never started so you won't have to deal with it stopping. Back in the day, the thrill of playing made you wish games would never end. Your youngblood fear and cockiness a high-octane, adrenaline rush only playing burns off. Hungry for the next game before the one you're playing's over. Always worried you won't get enough game. Then one day your beat-up body's begging for shortcuts, not more game, would phone ahead and cancel games if it could. Though your body whines and wags its nappy head, *huh-uh, no-no,* still some nights you don't want the game to be over. Wanting to play, wanting to be a star's got nothing to do with the feeling. What's up is fear. Maybe tonight your night to go down or, worse, your night to step off the court, out the arena's back gate, and fall, falling and falling, no sidewalk, no sparkling city out there under your feet.

On such a night Satterwhite, Archie Satterwhite, *the* Archie Satterwhite, the last player as usual left in the locker room besides me, tries one more time. Archie's my main man, we've been through it all together, so he tries to convince me one more time. Not tonight, Sat, I ain't hanging out tonight. Tired, man. My heart's not in it. You go on ahead without me, Sat. *Sat* an old nickname hardly anybody uses anymore. Nobody's allowed to use it except us few old heads who remember Sat's short for Sat-the-Bench, the teasing name tagging Archie his rookie year when an aging white hope kept Sat sitting instead of playing. No way Sat could hope to win the veteran's spot by virtue of talent, hard work, pure, unadulterated superiority in every facet of the game. So Sat sat the bench night after night till the white dude went down, and Sat an all-star every season since. Should have been all-league his first season except the sportswriters gave it to White Hope for old times' sake.

Sat hollers over his shoulder, What you mean you ain't hanging, man. Thanks, man. Thanks a fuck of a lot. What I'm spozed to do with two bitches.

Do these ladies have names.

Don't go getting cute now. Course the hoes got names. Lena and Rena.

Last names.

You hanging or not, man. Got no time to be messing wit

you. Told you it's Lena and Rena. Sisters. Or go for sisters. Or cousins. How the fuck am I spozed to know. Jackson. Johnson. Jefferson. Take your pick. Since when you been so particular about names. Take your pick.

Bet you already picked the fine one. Left me the bow-legged, wall-eyed little sister.

You know Sat wouldn't do nothing like that to his bro. Both ladies fine as wine.

Not tonight, Sat. I'm tired. Got a letter to write. Some reading I've been trying to get to.

Reading. I'm worried about you, blood. Reading. Letters. Shit. The night still young. Ladies all fired up. You getting old on me, man.

Instead of answering I stare at my feet. Think how strange they look in street shoes. Wonder why I bother with street shoes just to walk to the bus. Hear the locker room door wheeze open. Sat hovers an extra beat or two, giving me another chance.

Who's the one getting old, Sat. Once upon a time when you a young man, two ladies wouldn't have presented no problem to the Great Mr. Satterwhite.

After he slams the locker room door, after Archie Satterwhite crashes to the hardwood floor, after I toss and turn for hours too busted-up and road-weary to sleep and decide this season's my last go round the league, before I inch the final mile of waking up, I'm standing in a crowd alongside a freshly dug grave. A body wrapped in rags lies on a plank next to a deep hole in what I take to be red Mississippi clay. A gaping pit, blacker and blacker if you dare peep over the crusty edge, down, down into never-ending darkness. The people around me are Africans, brown men, women, children, a gang of strangers who are also, if I look closely at any one of the sad faces, a teammate or a person I've known my whole life. No one's lips move, but I hear a loud humming like millions and millions of bees or locusts whirring in the woods behind my grandfather's house in the country, where I used to be sent summer weekends to keep me out of city trouble. Or maybe the music plays only inside my skull like the goddamn tinnitis plaguing me. No sign the others beside the grave hear what I hear. But how can you ever know what somebody else is hearing or thinking. All you can do is ask, and if the other person bothers to answer, why would you believe he'd tell the truth. So I don't ask. Anyway, if these other people are Africans, and somehow I'm sure they are, how would they understand my question. What language, whose language, should we speak here, wherever *here* is. Wherever this impossible shit happens and drags in more strange stuff. I'm not in charge. This space belongs to someone older, smarter. Maybe the ancient, crippled-up grandfather of my grandfather. Babysitting that old, old man my grandpa's job when he was a boy in South Carolina. Watching his grandfather sleep, listening to his grandfather's stories, feeding him, tending his slop bucket. Maybe I'm listening to my great-great-grandfather remember a secret gathering of slaves in the woods, slaves in a circle chanting, returning one of their own to Africa or a place even more distant and older than Africa, an unnamable, desirable place none of us huddling around the grave will ever reach alive.

I'm changing. Happy to change, though I'm not sure why I'm happy about becoming a slave. Soon I'll remember my tribal name, the name of the dead traveler. I'll be able to pick out members of my clan from the crowd, speak to them. If none of my kin survived the raid on our village, the long, forced march in chains, the nightmare voyage across oceans, I'll begin here and now to fashion a new family. New flesh, bodies linked to mine, determined to soldier on with me in spite of how much we've been hurt, how much we've lost. Soon, soon, a pair of eyes set in one of these brown faces will catch a glint of light, fix me in a kinsman's all-seeing, welcoming smile. Or perhaps I'm the one who's on the ground, giving it up, my warm skin cooling, at last, at last, in the bundle of rags and the humming background noise an arena slowly drained of all its scurrying, scrambling occupants, the busy traffic of thousands of feet fleeing in many directions that is really the same direction, away, away, a termite mound emptying, like my body emptying, leaving me behind. Everybody gone and me left behind. Or everybody left behind and me gone. It could be happening. Must happen one day.

Goody-bye, goody-bye. What I read Africans used to say to spirits coming or going. What they chanted to send one of themselves back across the water with letters from survivors not quite ready to return. Africans flying home, Africans floating, skywalking and skyrunning the air of Georgia, Texas, Alabama, Tennessee, Arkansas. *Goody-bye, goody-bye.* Africans shapeshifting from one skin to another. Faster than the speed of light. I read that the message-bearer who's called home, sent home, must be silent. Only silence has room for the humming I'm hearing, room for cannons booming, flames roaring, room for the screams of the murdered, wailing of captives, room, room, and still more room to drown our sorrow while we circle this grave and still more room for messages we send to the other side. Room for a freshly fallen body and our weary bodies, room for words we're not ashamed to load on the dead's shoulders, the shoulders of the unborn, greetings, wishes, confessions we hope they will not be ashamed to repeat. An ocean of silence, untroubled, unmarked, lost-and-found room for everything, no matter how much noise, how many burdens we shovel into the hole.

That's why the fallen one must lie so still. With far to go, much to carry, a body must rest and rest. Where I stand, I can see myself watching. Not here. Not there. Not me. Not the one down. I'm present and absent. Motionless though time never stops. Falling. Falling slowly and everyone watching me fall, but I'll be the last to know. My scribbled words in the wrong language alongside ribbons, a bloody bandage, a lock of hair, salt, wildflowers, the leg of a toad, a crow's feather, bee's wing, leaves and sticks and stones others have smoothed, tucked, sprinkled, spit, rubbed on the winding cloth, our good news and bad news mailed home for eyes we'll never see, hands never touch, voices never hear.

Goody-bye, goody-bye. I see fish swimming across a plowed field. A pale worm sprouting wings and rising. Birdfish, fish-birds leaping, bodies arched like rainbows, their feathers or gills or hide or shell, whatever you'd call their wrappings for which there are no words, glisten, shimmer like metal, like wind, like water, thousands of messages, thousands of tiny faces climbing, row after row, from courtside to rafters, tiers of eyes circling the arena.

I'm catching on at last. In this unfolding space nothing stays what it appears to be. What happens is a door into itself, through itself, to something else. Like the hip clothes we profile sauntering into the arena. Like our flashy uniforms. Like our steaming, naked skin after we peel off sweaty gear, toss it on a pile for someone to wash whiter than snow. Like the dead. Like the fallen one we cover with our messages, our chanting. Dressing him, hiding him.

I'm no less a stranger here even though I can account for some of the strangeness. Not the mixed blessing of déjà vu. More like I've been prepared by voices that know how to grab my attention, even though, like my grandfather, they speak barely above a whisper and not often. The scene's not exactly meaningless, not quite crazy: the fallen one could be Sat or Sat in drag or a stranger wearing a Sat mask calling me, teasing me, C'mon, Negro, the night's still young. Sat hesitates at the locker room doorway. I can't not look. He starts to lift his mask and I cringe. Expect a horror show of bloody meat, drool, pus, veins, sinews. What I get is Sat's voice: Maybe it's me, bro, maybe not, but your boon coon Sat's with you, bro, part of this shit, always, don't you forget. Then I see past whatever Sat's pretending to be, see Sat's hidden features pressed up against the back of the mask, breathing through nose holes, mouth hole, hear him suck his teeth, watch the big, bald, bowling ball head wagging Sat's wag.

One by one, my brother, Sat says. Going down one by one. Faster and faster. Soon won't be none us leff. Nobody speaking de ole language. Nobody wit de ole moves. Going down one by one, baby. Poor baby. *Goody-bye, goody-bye.* Ain't it what dese funny-looking niggers, I mean African sisters and brothers, be saying. *Goody-bye.* Won't be none us leff in a minute.

Sweat darkens Sat's uniform. A puddle spreading under him, a black hole he's dived in and ain't never coming back.

Here comes the little rooster of a referee with the basketball tucked tight under his wing so nobody will run up behind him and pull one of those corny old Globetrotter reams — steal the ball and eat it or change it to a bucketful of water and douse the fans with confetti. He squeezes through the circle, whispers in the coach's ear. Coach nods and the ref in his zebra shirt and last season's black stretch pants with not enough stretch for this year's butt and belly heads for the official's table to make sure no one cheats up the score during the break. Or maybe this once he'll blim-blim, bling-bling over to the scorekeeper and order more time on the clock, or less time, whatever it takes to erase the terrible fall.

Tomorrow everybody will say they knew it was coming, but nobody knew shit till the moment Sat landed. Still don't know shit. Hear people tell the story you'd think Sat's fall a replay. Like been there, done that. Like no big thing, seen it a hundred times before. Like they're connected and get the news beforehand so nothing surprises them. But the game goes on and on, not one game repeated — more game, different game, always. Always news. No playback or fast-forward or time out. Game doesn't end when somebody falls. For a moment you might think so and study the one who's down. Could be you, but you still won't know shit.

My grandfather had a shotgun and hunted birds and that's what I thought of when Sat fell. A bird high up flying fast and then *pow*, bird drops like a stone. Knuckle crack of bone split on the shiny floor. Sat's long, dark body not moving. Damn. *Didn't believe the old boy could still hop that high.* Sat's glazed eyes staring at nothing we're able to see. The hushed arena kneels, leans in closer for a peek, for a listen.

We tighten our circle, seal the gap where the ref slipped through. Part of our job. We're pros, paid for holding on and letting go, winning and losing, good news and bad news. Who cares. Just as long as we get paid. Just so everybody feels safe. And for the moment everybody is, except the one down. Who we love because we're not him. And love standing around for a couple of minutes with nothing harder to do than worry about how we look, wishing our big shorts had pockets to hide our big hands.

In the same fat book where I read about slave burials I learned *down* is not necessarily bad. Some Africans believe down's holy, one of the Four Kingdoms of the Sun. Without down no up, no world. The sun must rest every day so these African people carve fancy stools for kneeling and watching the sun drop into the sea. Double sun for a while, one in the sky, its twin shining on the water, then half a sun as it sinks, then no sun it seems, just brightness bleeding, spreading, blinding you, scaring you because the sun might not rise again, and for a heartbeat the gold fire really does seem to die. You can almost hear the sizzle. You worry that the sun's too heavy, heavier even than the steel-boned arena kneeling behind our backs, so how will it get its big self up off the floor. The sun will drown. Night never end. But down's not out, the Africans say. Sun sleeps faster than the speed of light. Shoots through the thick earth, pops out the other side still burning if you're awake next morning to see it. So down can't be all bad. The sun bends down and warms water swallowing it. People bend their knees to pray, to dance, to jump up and fly. To get down.

How long. How long will this stranger, this messenger dropped from the sky, stay down. We don't know the answer, can't set our faces right. How long will he cover for us. When will our safe moment end. Who goes down next. If the teammate stretched out on the floor doesn't answer these questions we load on him, who will. How long will it take our messages to cross the sea. How long before play starts up again. All the things we wish to know swirl in the chanting. All we can't know thickens it.

In my fat book, on one of the back pages lined with four columns of tiny print describing full-page illustrations, I found some information about Plate 124, a human figure carved from ebony, a person who could have been normal-sized once, maybe even taller than a basketball player, but some god or devil had sneaked up behind the guy and dumped the whole world's weight on him, squashed him so he looked like three blubbery lips, pancaked one on top the other. Head, belly, and butt blobs you could tell because arrowheads of braid zippered the head blob, a navel poked in the belly blob, elephant toes etched on the bubble-butt blob which rested on the ground.

Talk about a brother being down. Talk about burdens bowing a bro's shoulders. This African man or woman, both since anything anybody could be all squeezed together, glowed black on the white page, smooth, shiny as a bowling ball. Could be a bowling ball. Just needed finger holes, a little more rounding, squashing, to be perfect for bowling. And you know you can always find people willing and happy to do the dirty work. Turn us into something useful. Squeeze some more. Peel our skin, burn it black. Bore holes. Ask Emmett Till. Ask James Byrd, Malcolm, Martin. Check out your children. Check around your own body, sisters and brothers, for fingerprints. For work-in-progress.

Mene, mene, tekel, upharsin. The other afternoon walking into work I glanced up and noticed some Spiderman terrorist had climbed the arena and tagged the dome's brow. Somebody must believe the building's dead. Wants to launch the big, dumb, flying-saucer arena back to sender, back to outer space, with a warning from the Book of Daniel: *The days of the empire are numbered. Mene. Mene. Tekel.* Aramaic from the Old Testament. The strange words spray-painted up there sounded like music when I tried them out loud. Many, many tinkle. Tinkle. Tinkle. A bouncy pop tune. The kind of ear worm you keep hearing over and over in your mind even when you don't want to. Like a headache, like tinnitis. *Mene, tekel.* Like turnstiles clicking. Money. Money. Fans piling in to watch us play. Tinkle, tinkly music blasting through the PA system before a game. Tekel of turnstiles clicking. Shiny shekels piling up. Tonight's gimmick a bar of Ivory soap with each ticket purchased. Our team's going to *clean up* this season. Clean up our act and go straight to the top. Number one. Ninety-nine and forty-four-one-hundredths percent pure like the Deep Throat Ivory Soap lady says. A promotion to end all promotions. Bring the whole family. If you buy enough tickets, soap forever. Clean forever. Step right up to the shower. Who doesn't want to be pure and clean clear through. Who doesn't want to win and win.

Beware, beware the gulf of Benin / Few come out / Many go in. Sailors sang that sea shanty, but nobody listened.

I watch old Sat-the-Bench, tipsy, sore with arthritis, rise and leave the circle. Below the string tied round his neck Sat ain't got no secrets as he hobbles away from us, hospital gown flapping open around his hips, billowing up to his armpits, gone with the wind. He gingerly steps into a puddle of sea a wave's left behind, another wave on its way. Oh my, my. Like old, blind Oedipus, Sat's not the strength he once was. Thin shanks, scored behind, bent back. Seeking sanctuary. Oh shit, Sat. Did you just wiggle your sorry booty. Did you flash your middle finger or was it two fingers signing V. Is that loose skin, dem dry bones just another disguise. Are you still playing games. Messing wit my head.

Sea rises to Sat's crusty ankles. Don't go. Don't go, I holler, loud as I can into the wind. The circle breaks up. My words splash like they hit a wall and rebound icy, salty in my face.

Never again. The first words a player says when we notice there's no one in the space we've been guarding.

Never again. Our messages, buzzing and swarming like flies above the damp spot where Sat hit, look at us like we're crazy. Like they just might change their minds and go nowhere. Like we should know better than to speak the two words they've just heard. *Never again.* Roll their eyes as if to say, Right. Tell me about it. Play on.

Sightings

T HE FIRST TIME it happened I could forgive myself for
being confused. Cutting across the hall from my office
into the departmental office and glimpsing a man — pale, wearing metal-rimmed glasses, a thin man in a light-colored, rolled-
sleeved shirt and khaki pants, busy with files he was returning
or extricating from a chin-high bank of beige metal cabinets
lining the wall to my right, just inside the departmental office
. . . nothing unforgivable about being confused a split second
by the sight of someone I knew was dead, dead a good long
while, dead and buried two thousand miles away in cold,
high Wyoming, the dead man Roger Wilson's office down and
across from mine, fourth floor Bartlett Hall, the dozen years I'd
taught at UW, so countless times I'd caught him hunched over
his desk under a window opposite the door he always left
slightly ajar or him standing, puttering in his share of the ubiquitous metal file cabinets that graced Bartlett and also preside
here in this English department located in a building I find myself sometimes calling Bartlett, or rather find myself unable to
recall this building's name once Bartlett pops into my head,
even after ten years of coming and going through this building's
glass vestibule and thick double doors, one with a push button
and ramp for handicap access, nothing unusual or shameful
about seeing dead Roger Wilson and silently calling out his
name, surprised, hopeful, though I knew better than to believe
I'd actually seen him, so I could easily forgive myself for being
lost in space and spacing out a present colleague's name, turn-

ing him into a ghost too, who floated invisible above the figure in round bifocals, manila folders in hand, crouching over an open file drawer, my present colleague a phantom whose name I could not say though I struggled like a stutterer to push his name out, it wouldn't descend from the shelf in my brain where it was stored, technical difficulties, transmission temporarily interrupted, the flesh-and-bone body I was staring at could not belong to dead Roger Wilson who'd canceled his claim to a body long ago with a shotgun blast and become a lost soul, visible in this office only to me unless someone could enter my skull, pick their way through the mess of overflowing drawers, files, stacked newspapers, bags of trash, like after a foul odor summons cops to bust through a locked door and they find a recluse rotting on a mattress walled in by debris in a corner of his flat, if you could reach the place in my mind from which Roger Wilson had suddenly appeared, you wouldn't blame me, might forgive me as easily as I forgive myself for mixing up names, places, the living and dead, because it could happen to anyone, happens frequently and usually passes without comment, it's so ordinary and startling at the same time, people figure it's not worth mentioning, who else would want to hear about such an inconsequential moment of slippage, who will attend your funeral, the party for your retirement or publication of your first novel, let alone care whether you are mixed up an instant about the identity of a man you glimpse out of the corner of your eye, a split second of confusion leading nowhere except in a heartbeat back to the commonplace reality of a Tuesday, late in the afternoon, post-seminar, post a dawn commute from New York City to the university in Massachusetts where I've landed and stuck since leaving the mountain West, obviously exhausted and stressed from the long day of travel and teaching when I step cattycorner across the hall and there's old schoolmarm lean and severe, great white hunter and sorry-ass alcoholic, my buddy Roger, wasting his good mind and precious time as usual futzing with files, documenting the shamefully low graduation rate of minority student athletes or serving as liaison between physical sciences and humanities for an interdisciplinary, crosscultural project of team teaching or organizing a new, socially relevant concentration perhaps one day a major, a department where now there is none, its absence or presence a ghost agitating the fertile, slightly hungover brain of my former colleague who's risen from the grave to occupy — yes, yes, I'm able to say the name now — a place here in *Logan Hall,* then just as quickly relinquishes it, fades, and that's *Charley* staring at me, Charley Morin, puzzled because he's caught me staring, an unconventionally long and thus suspect pause, our eyes locked and neither of us offering an explanation, an awkward silence I interrupt finally to clear the air, to sweep away the indecision that must have emptied my gaze of expression and caused Charley perhaps to feel vaguely responsible, perhaps challenged, minding his own business, then sensing the weight of eyes on his bony shoulders, he turns, meets an undecipherable look with a quizzical tilt of his head, his eyes invisible behind thick lenses whose steel rims catch fire as he straightens, shoot a silver tracer to the ceiling, the crimson afterimage slowly deforming in the air, and I recall the words *pillars of light* I heard first coming from the mouth of a physicist and vice president at the University of Wyoming who was attempting to explain to me during intermission at a lunch meeting something beautiful and eerie I reported observing one night camped out in the Snowies, a mountain range with year-round white peaks thirty miles or so east of Laramie, same mountains where Roger Wilson was discovered splattered inside the locked cab of his red pickup after he'd been missing six days, *pillars of light* a nice, evocative phrase I'd thought for the effect produced by rare, spectacular conspiracies of light, temperature, moisture, and wind above high plains plateaus like the one Laramie rests upon, *pillars of light* a poetic image startling me in the faculty dining room nearly as much as I'd been startled by vertical shafts of oscillating brightness striating the night horizon, especially since the vice president who said *pillars of light* usually spoke in a bluff, clipped fashion, pedestrian to a notorious extreme, but as I crunched on my chicken salad sandwich, recalling a time when I couldn't stomach chicken or tuna salad with celery in it, recalling torrents of unsatisfactory words running through my head that night in the mountains, pretending to listen to my colleagues, you know, the way you can look and not look, the phrase *pillars of light* continued to echo and I became less grateful for the vice president's assistance, then his figure of speech collapsed and I saw poor bloody Samson, heard the temple crashing down around his shoulders after he snapped its marble columns, but I wasn't blind, I watched the words *pillars of light* disintegrate, or rather the letters lifting and reshuffling themselves, each letter like a person unshackled from an old life, letters quivering in a kind of jerky, cartoony dance, funny almost, like Molly described letters and numbers detaching from license plates, scrambled letters hanging in the air, jiggly, silly, she said, if you didn't know what the letters would do next, snap into place abrupt as a door slamming to spell out a command she must follow, she said, no matter how stupid or dangerous or humiliating she must do what the letters ordered and *Gawd,* she said, you can't imagine the godawful trouble I'd get into, the trouble afterward trying to explain crazy stuff to myself or explain it to my mom or Sarah or the shrink or any stranger who'd listen, she said, smiling, the worst once when my job sent me to Africa to sell barbed wire and steel fenceposts and I loved Africa, loved the people, really enjoying myself over there and learning so much, then I wake up in a cruddy hotel in Ouagadougou, I found out later, in a bed in some dark little hot smelly room, no idea how I got there, where I was, who I was, how long, just lying there bareass naked remembering one sweaty black guy after another pounding away inside me, no faces, no names, just hands pulling and poking and pinching, it could have been going on for days, I stunk like a skunk, man, drugged probably, hurt so badly I'd stopped feeling pain, fear, anything, blacked out I guess, didn't even know my name till I heard Mom's voice Molly Molly like she used to whisper tickling and shaking my shoulder, *Molly, dear, it's time for school,* that hotel room the worst, man, she said, smiling, the two of us in Boston at an outdoor Au Bon Pain table, craziness a different planet she visited occasionally, once upon a time, okay, many times, she smiled again, a faraway place, like not plugged into this one, she says, her bare arms opening wide to embrace sunny afternoon streets busy with shoppers, blond, hard-bodied Molly, bright-eyed, tan that last day I'd see her before she too killed herself, her hands betrayed only the vaguest tremor performing the magic of transforming water to tea, safe because she'd been taking her medicine daily, not skipping doses though the poison zombied her some days, enough good days, clear hours like this one I'd caught her in so she continues to pop a purple, elephant-sized pill each morning, See, she says, holding up one extricated from a small deerskin purse lavishly fringed like the deerskin jacket I'd passed down to her, unstylishly tight on me, tons too large for Molly but she loved it, her trademark a fringed teepee draping her from early adolescence through her teens till it just about fit her broad swim-team shoulders, Look how big, and I'm naked again in the ruins, a huge black Wyoming sky over my head, a sky filled with streamers of bright blood, the wakes of slow-motion falling stars, funnels of pale fire wavering above a bombed-out city burning just beyond the next mountain's dark crest, no words, no made-up names would do, each time I looked up I was stunned by distance, by silence, no words for the raw power destabilizing me. Was order or chaos striping the sky. Neither. Both. Why did beauty scare me, why does strangeness threaten, hello-goodbye, dead Roger Wilson, goodbye, hi, Charley, excuse me for staring, man, but when I bopped through the door I had a flashback, you know, a weird kind of time wobble and it wasn't you in the corner of my eye over there but some other guy in another place another time, and damn, for a second it had me going, very real, real and very odd, you know what I mean, it shook me up, and Charley's face crinkles, no more needs to be said by either of us, just a minute's worth of wannabe super-witty and hip banter, spread like thick, gooey icing over a hopeless cake, like exchanges with Roger if he responded to the silence of my footsteps stopping or the stealth of my glance trespassing the space he'd left open for just that purpose or when we'd bump into each other in the hall, *bump* a foolish word like *jump*, as in *jump* in the shower, both words untrue, their embedded metaphors describing events that don't occur, acts unperformed, fictions, as in I was *touched* by his gentleness, or *ran into* an old friend, or *touched* by the pain of his wife and kids, *moved* by her struggle, *touched* by a sudden, senseless suicide.

I hadn't thought much about Roger or Molly for years. For some reason never paired them, though they knew each other well and were linked by the obvious fact of suicide. I'd been long gone from Wyoming when I heard they'd taken their lives, Roger first, then Molly, each death a kind of postscript to a portion of my life I thought I'd laid to rest until these painful footnotes forced me to raise my eyes to a text that hadn't disappeared just because I'd stopped reading it.

Let's just say, without specifying why or which one, a hunting party in the Snowies fits here, now, in a blank space I need to fill, the ground giving way beneath my feet, no warning, the wet snow instead of packing hard under my strides goes mushy and *oh shit* I start to slide and might not ever stop. Always winter and white when I remember hunting in the mountains, though once a preseason scouting outing at the end of July, only month you can be nearly certain it won't snow, the old-timers say, hot July days and the high country perfect as Eden, the Alibi Bar crew with families tagging along, a big camp pitched on the bank of a stream, yes, cleansed and starting over is how it felt on that summer weekend I didn't expect to surface here, my wife and kids, borrowed tent and sleeping bags, finding bones on a hike with my two boys, whole lot of bleached bones scattered on a flat boulder at the mouth of a cave we decided had to be a cougar's den, sunlight polishing stones that bedded the talking stream, at night absolute blackness inside our tent, old canvas funky as a gym, everybody blind, whispering as we settled down to sleep, the tent could be empty or full, you needed to touch to see, your own hand invisible until it gropes out someone.

No, not that July. Let it go. I'm trekking through serious snow, high-stepping into someone else's deep tracks. I don't want to discover a bottomless drift or treacherous crevice or the thin ice of a black-hole lake hidden just below the snow, ever-present possibilities up here, especially in spring when the season seems to change after you slog thigh-deep in snow for a mile then topping a rise see a meadow below scoured clean except for frozen puddles of whiteness with dark stubble poking through or dried swirls of snow trapped here and there in coils of spiky sagebrush. I'm not alone. Had been warned against it — tales of foolish people, their bones picked clean by the time a hiker stumbles over them in May — so I never tried the Snowies alone in winter. Didn't own a four-wheel drive anyway to get me close enough once passes barricaded in November. Not alone, not able to say whom I'm with. Could be my best buddy John, rifle cradled in his arms, out there on point plowing ahead of me, John's tracks my boots trace, or I could be with Alex and Sarah, Molly's older sister, or with brown Chris and Harry or white Max, Walt, Fred, Herb, and John again, the Alibi Bar crew, each group distinct, every person a small-town character of sorts with his or her story you wouldn't hear in the Snowies since hunting parties organized so nobody would have to tell their tale, nobody have to listen. A particular chemistry and energy defined each combination of personalities, yet as I look back, one group blurs into the other. Only fragments return, random bits and pieces effortlessly more real than this fading present. Details I can hear, see, touch, smell, taste, my senses so sure of themselves they expect more, desire more, but there is no center. I'm here, not in Wyoming, and each promising detail bodiless, the network of memories it spins out cannot hold, evaporates, brings back everything, nothing.

Hunting simplifies and clarifies like war. Pleases like war. Not only because humans are predators who enjoy stalking and killing. In fact, for the hunters I knew the fun seemed less in killing than in getting ready to kill. Imagining themselves killing. Gathering their hunting gear. Anticipating themselves dressed to kill. Lies afterward about kills that never happened. All of it — beginning with purchase of a license in September at the little Fish and Game shed behind Albertson's in West Laramie — frees them. Hunters can't wait for the season to start, but they must, and waiting's a welcome clock counting down their ordinary lives, rendering everyday duties slightly less demeaning.

It's no coincidence that hunts begin in the hour of the wolf. In the *taint* — taint night, taint day, taint neither one, so it's just *taint*. Town left behind, hunters shamble along in semilight, semidark, grumpy, surly, not speaking if grunt or gesture will do. Play at being animals. Beg for the animal's complicity. Hope the animals love them as much as they love the animals. Hunters wish they lived in the mountains. Wish they could devour human trespassers. Beasts *and* men. Hunters *and* hunted. As if they have a choice. As if they can remain both. As if it's not death but miraculous exchange waiting in the mountains. As if, like kids playing war, they can squeeze the trigger, then holler and crumple in slow motion, have fun groaning and twisting on the ground after their bullets strike.

Of course it doesn't work that way. We're always the hunted. At the moment of truth, when the coincidence of hunter and hunted occurs, we don't possess the writer's prerogative to sort out who's who and decide where the story's going.

In a small, isolated town like Laramie — maybe anywhere you reside long enough to establish the routine of your habits — you become unbearably transparent. People look through you. Your presence confirms the town's presence, the town's bottomless capacity to level and consume. A town's gaze — its curiosity about my color, my pretensions to write a novel, for instance — never innocent. It's sizing up the lump it intends to swallow. Hey, how you doing and go away, leave me alone. Love and hate in one quick, hungry, breakaway glance.

You can go a little insane trying to find something new about yourself. Try on a different life to convince yourself one might exist just beyond the horizon of familiar routines. You take up a hobby, steal a chocolate bar from Albertson's, screw your best buddy's wife, or you drive up into the Snowies, lock yourself into your pickup, and blow out your brains with a shotgun, or run away and fatten up in another Wyoming feedlot town, snuff out your life one day like Molly snuffed hers I can't even say how.

But you can't inch closer to what's unreachable. The unknown remains precisely that — unknown. All those tabloid descriptions of near-death experiences bullshit because no pilgrim has returned and reported how it feels to die. You can't grasp the unknown even when it's pissing in your face. That's the dirty joke hunters go to the mountains to laugh at. Werewolf with other werewolves, furry clothes, furry faces, stomachs bloated with jelly doughnuts and beer.

Though certain scenes are attached indelibly to one group or another — high-butt Chris's long-legged country-boy strides in no hurry as they tirelessly consume miles of rugged terrain, Harry's head bobbing and weaving, his ghetto shoulder swagger efficiently stylized so he keeps pace side by side with Chris in open country or pushes out when his turn to cut trail through deep snow, Sarah shivering, a blue Michelin lady, the chubby arms of her parka hugging the jacket's roly-poly bulk, her eyes pleading, demanding an answer, and when I have none she stares at Alex, silhouetted on the next ridge, his fine brain at half mast since the day it bounced helmetless along a dirt road for twenty yards beyond his overturned Suzuki, blue-eyed Alex emptying his rifle, pow-pow-pow-pow, slowly, methodically, into a pocket meadow where a dozen or so pronghorns had been browsing, spooked and long gone before he got off his first shot — these scenes, distinct as the crack of a Coors opened at dawn in the mountains, also blend into one seamless hunt, a work-in-progress, everybody out there still wandering the Snowies, me bowing my head as near as I can get to the roots of a solitary clump of dwarf pines, last trees before we climb too high for trees, kneeling so I can hear what sounds like a fast river a mile underground or the fierce, baffled moaning and whistling of a windstorm miniaturized within tangles of brush and skinny tree trunks the way the sea echoes in a shell clamped to your ear, kneeling, listening, amazed by the black roots' howl but I can't say who told me to kneel, can't say why I feel ambushed by coincidence.

Imagine seeing a familiar face forming in a bank of clouds or an incredible mix of color, light, and motion blazing on the horizon. Imagine needing someone who will recognize the face or amen the sunset, but you're sure that if you turn away to find someone, when you turn back, with or without your witness, the sky will have changed.

Last week a flock of honking Canada geese suddenly passed over my head, so low I felt their wind, the chill of their fluttering shadow spreading over me, a net that just might snatch me wherever they were flying, remembering only after the geese had disappeared that I'd heard them startled up by I don't know what from a pond near the road I was jogging on, the clatter, splash, and panicked cries of their lifting, their wake strong enough to whiplash the pond, decapitate me if I didn't duck fast.

One day I see Roger in the department office, next day Molly's voice over the phone. A day or so after, on my next commute to UMass, I overhear a blond woman on the train yammering excitedly to her cell phone about foxes in the woods behind her house, red foxes — one standing guard, the other, one cub at a time in her mouth, moving to a new den. No idea foxes back there, she exclaims, and then one, two, a whole cute little fox family . . . and I see Molly's orphaned baby fox, crazier each day she tries to keep it for a pet, dart red under her mom's new sofa, nip blood from Molly's finger with its tiny needle teeth when she tries to scoop it out.

I don't believe past explains present, nor present explains past, and certainly coincidence doesn't explain anything, but peculiar, disruptive spaces I'm calling *coincidences,* for want of a better word, open almost daily. Past and present chat, maybe, or maybe refuse to speak to each other, who knows, but their convergence seems to uncover crucial information just beyond my grasp. At these moments my life feels crowded and empty. I'm stalled at a crossroads with lots of traffic in many directions whirring around me and I can't regain my bearings, don't know how to step back into the flow.

Molly Ritello, who's never called in the ten years we've been colleagues at UMass, phoned me at home. John . . . hello, John. It's me, Molly . . . the voice not belonging here, an unmistakable sore-throat huskiness, a nasal twang at the ends of words and phrases, singsong almost, the pixels of it visibly wobbly, as if forming words a precarious business, not to be taken for granted, a girl's voice trying on adult sound effects, pumping itself up with grown-up bluster, sentences chipping away at the edges of what she's meaning to articulate, just give her a little time and patience, the young-forever voice of Molly, my first Molly high up in a tree I'm standing at the foot of while she climbs, agile as a monkey, me the adult on duty in the back yard to watch her, to caution and slow her, catch her if need be, sent to do the job by her anxious mom, martini in hand at the kitchen's French doors, Christina in a goofy tuxedo apron watching me watch her Molly climb, my eyes with no choice except to fix themselves on Molly's round little bottom, the white cotton drawers, twist of glen-plaid skirt, her bare legs as they scissor and stretch up the gnarled tree's rungs to a shelf near the top she and Sarah call the Fairy Queen throne, Molly's tight, neat buns years later when I get up to pee at 3:00 A.M. and catch her walking naked back down the hallway connecting bathroom to guest room to her and Sarah's room and she doesn't miss a step, proud I'm sure of her taut athlete's body, unselfconscious about my eyes as she'd been at ten scampering up a tree, and though neither of us utters a word, she knows I'm behind her, probably guesses I'm hung over from all the margaritas and wine knocked back with her mom and John and I guess she might be half asleep, probably still half stoned because it's a weekend and she'd split the grownup slooshing early for her own partying, she knows I'm there in the hall and knows her young woman's body glows in the darkness, knows I can't help seeing, appraising, admiring her and it's okay, fine, she likes the accident, the coincidence, understands how it might please me she says in the look she flashes over a bare shoulder, isn't that what she's telling me with her slow strides, the casual slap, slap of naked feet on the tile, saying, Yes, I'm a woman now, I've caught up with your being a man, and it's kinda nice, huh, hello, goodbye, let's get some sleep, Molly gone before I'm positive whom I've seen, gone though her pale shape hovers after her door clicks shut, Molly gone but not before I understand, stopped there in the darkness, that the moment stirred me and shouldn't have, and why does that moment come back, Molly's young, naked body like Roger's pained face returning here, now, as if nothing else about either of them mattered, my failures, guilt, my dead greeting me, testing me, reminding me there won't be another time, not with Molly, not with Roger, no second chance to do better, to do more than watch, never more than one time, one chance, and maybe once way more than enough, wouldn't I choose every time to be whoever I thought I wanted to be instead of friend or guardian, an unforgiving once, as if a father borrowed once and only once for three seconds the eyes of his daughter's brand-new groom beholding the perfect naked female creature the father had loved into the world, Hi, John, Molly here . . . speaking from the grave and I didn't dare answer. It's me, Molly, she says again and I'm on the other end of the line listening, unable to speak, green socks all I can think of, green socks and wanting to ask Molly what she'd done with them, green socks to match green blazer and green glen-plaid skirt, knee socks rolled down to her ankles when she climbed the tree or did you race off the school minivan directly into the room you shared with Sarah, chuck the monogrammed blazer across your bed, snatch the green tie from around your neck, plop down and whip off socks and shoes, or were you wearing shoes, am I making up curly white monkey toes gripping rough bark like fingers, Sure, I'll phone Jim — soon as we hang up — Thursday at 10:00, right, in your office — Thanks for setting everything up, and thanks for calling — See you Thursday. I don't remember how the conversation with Molly Ritello ended, what I've written above close enough, but I do remember saying to dead Molly's mother, *Done deal.* You keep an eye out for mine, I'll keep an eye out for yours, meaning whichever one survived the other would be an unofficial guardian of the dead friend's kids. I'd said those exact words, *Done deal,* and have wondered about them since. Christina's girls around nine and eleven, my boys four and six when we exchanged our little vow. A lighthearted, hugging, feel-good reassurance at the time, the kids young and we felt young too, maybe younger with the pledge between us that seemed to guarantee a certain immortality as much as it acknowledged the possibility of fatal accidents, because Christina and I, as well as the partners we spoke for, expected lots more life ahead, natural and full life, more or less owed to us, and now even in the unlikely event one of us might be struck down, the others would be left standing, a permanent safety net for the worst circumstances.

When we promised to be kind, responsible uncle or aunt to the other's children, was there an unspoken statute of limitations. Weren't we released or at least absolved from our obligations once the others' kids were grownups, out in the world on their own. By the point Molly's life began to fall apart, both couples had split and Molly more parent than child, orchestrating an intervention and commitment to rescue her mom from drinking herself to death, then nursing Christina through the last terrible stages of cancer. A few letters, phone calls—Oh, I'm okay. Just a teensy bit nuts sometimes is all. You know. All the lies get to me and crazy is a better place to be. You know. Mom's lies, the God lies, my so-called friends lying, our so-called leaders lying and murdering people, and you know I'm kinda glad in a way I don't see you much anymore, man, cause I bet you'd lie too. Crazy's better. Till I get sick of me crazy and want the lies again.

Except for a meeting when both of us happened to be in Boston, no contacts or news for years at a time—spared the awful metamorphosis, Christina shrinking down to nothing, Molly ballooning. The distance so huge I could only nod my head and ask myself how the fuck did it happen when John told me on the phone he'd heard Molly weighed over two hundred pounds.

Why do we let each other go, why do we watch, take what we can get as long as we can get it, till it's gone or can't be taken any longer, watching all this happening, then let go and try to forgive ourselves or at least comfort ourselves with the thought that most people are not much better at this than we are, they watch, take, let go, and in time it will be our turn to be let go, the others watching, forgetting, regretting. What's done is done, how could it have been any other way, we say. Then some unforgiving moment, some coincidence with no mercy sneaks up and announces the different way things could be. And it's as if two threads of time are trying to squeeze through the same needle's eye at once, but it's not separate threads, is it, always the same thread that only seems to divide into past and present, then and now because we need to believe we didn't take, didn't watch, didn't let go, need to believe what's done is done, no matter how true our witness of exactly the opposite.

A night ago a train erupted just inches from the one I was riding from Massachusetts to New York City and the train hurtling past in the opposite direction licked away the glowing carful of passengers I'd been studying in the darkness outside my train's window, all those faces, including my own, smashed and speeding away in the bright cage of the other train.

Will I glance up one day and see the huge Wyoming sky, find myself surrounded by the raw gorgeousness of daunting moonscape desolation, not for one forgivable instant, no déjà vu or daydream or miscalculation, but find myself there again, not a ghost like the ghosts of Wyoming sometimes haunting me here but there in Wyoming, stuck again as I'm stuck here, shopping for groceries at Albertson's, walking Harney or Grand, beer, bluegrass, and pool with John and Roger in the Cowboy Bar and Roger blows his quarter, scratching on an easy eight ball in the side pocket and that familiar wince of incredible disappointment pinches his features and I want to tell him it's okay, you're a good man, Roger, a very smart, very talented person I respect, everybody respects, though you'd be the last to hear it from them, don't always be so goddamned disappointed with the world, man, disappointed with yourself for failing to change it, my friend, or at least try being less visibly disappointed and maybe people won't assume you're blaming them for a world so evilly out of control, but I say instead what everybody around him says, Nice shot.

I anticipate a horrible stench. Steel myself not to gag, not to give the others an excuse to laugh in my face, snicker behind my back. The others my companions for a hunting party, John, Roger, Max, Herb, Walt, all of us up before dawn, rendezvousing outside the Alibi, dark empty roads like tunnels, then trudging miles through fresh snow they happily agree makes tracking easier and the going tougher, my companions who know I'm over thirty and have never stalked, shot, or gutted game, and they can't wait for me, the tag-along city kid, to lose my cool, fuck up, the black boy from Pittsburgh and Philly and New York where snow falls as white as Wyoming snow but does not stay white long, cities with gray skies from which these others, once upon a time, had tumbled, boys like me except they fled West to stay white as snow, all of them armed with a thirty-aught-six high-powered rifle, a handgun, a large knife, a Swiss Army pocket wad of blades for every purpose. Two guys smoking cigarettes, one chewing tobacco, one sipping a Coors from an endless six-pack cached in the bulk of his camouflage hunting vest. Roger steps away to pee. Smoke unwinds over his shoulder. Still zipping, he cuts a loud belch as he turns.

Forget it, Roger. No matter how crudely you act or talk up here, no matter how many notches on your gun or spots on your slovenly khakis or how much grime under your fingernails, you'll never fit in — too much Eastern prep school, too much Eng. Lit. professor whose existence insults the others even as you dispense a desired patina of knowledge and culture, red-pencil their B/B– essays, too much stern, thin-lipped, narrow-hipped spinster, New England rectitude and ruling class and old money, money proved by your poor churchmouse lifestyle, your disdain for stuff other folks work their tails off to own. Then I show up in Laramie — a suspicion, a gut feeling in the others that somehow you're responsible — a brown professor in Bartlett Hall who reminds them of their crimes, flight, waywardness, failure to measure up.

They say animals trapped with you in your truck. Smell sucked them in — they couldn't get out. Looked like the goddamn OK Corral in there.

What's so bad about poaching, Wilson. You ought to run for sheriff, my man.

You know goddamned well sheriff's not elected.

Right. But Wilson ought to run anyway. If he's the only candidate, might just win.

Hell, yeah. You got all the Alibi votes. Herb here would sponsor you, wouldn't you, Herb. Good for business. Move the sheriff's office to the Alibi.

Where you going, dear. Oh, I'd love to sit home and watch soaps with you, honey, but I got pressing business over at the sheriff's office.

Shouldn't be a hunting season. Should run it like we do at the county hospital now. Morphine hooked up to an IV so patients can medicate themselves. As needed. Makes more sense in every way to me. Hunting as needed. Problem's not poaching, anyway. Folks round here don't kill for killing's sake. For some of these hods, a big buck in August the difference between meat and no meat on the table come fall.

Bet Mr. Tenderfoot here agrees with old Tenderfoot Wilson, don't you. Save the animals. Shit's sake, no shortage of animals. Would have seen for yourself, my man, if you'd been around the year of the big blizzard. Snow piled up thirty foot deep in the mountains. Game couldn't forage so they started sneaking into town. Shock at first. A wild critter where you don't expect to see one. Then before you know it, a goddamned invasion. Antelope deer elk moose jackalope. Like some damned Noah's ark. Like goddamn welfare. Bunches of 'em trooping down from the mountains around dusk looking for a handout. Hung round the golf course at first, then started parading in the streets like they owned them. Breaking and entering people's barns. Stealing what folks had stored up for livestock. Turning over garbage cans, drinking out the town fountain. Shit's sake. Clomp right in your front door if it wasn't locked. Plague of cussed animals. Turned the dogs on 'em. Dogs got fat and lazy feeding on the carcasses. Didn't slow the critters up one bit. Had to see it to believe it. Critters and carcasses everywhere. Blizzard wiped out half the herd, still plenty left to do mischief. Hell, had to elbow your way through critters to get up to the bar.

Walt's got a point. No shortage of animals. Plenty critters even without tenderhearted Sheriff Wilson here protecting their rights.

Damned straight I got a point. Why do you think nature crops them. If not, they'd eat us out of house and home. Then eat each other. So why not pop one when you feel a need to pop one. A kindness, really.

The others a veteran crew, regulars from the Alibi abiding the presence of an eternal rookie, extra baggage along for the ride, for a joke. No gun, no intention to kill anything would set me apart, if nothing else, from my companions semicircled around John in his grease-monkey coveralls. He's dropped down to one knee beside a gut-shot antelope whose bad dying he's just terminated with a pointblank bullet to the brain from his pistol.

I remember the ground under John's knee. Ground antelope color, or the antelope the color of ground it had staggered across, barely able to hold up its pronghorned head, slow, faltering steps, neck bowing lower and lower, the antelope weary, maybe ashamed of surrender, of helplessness, aiming for the rifle held by a baggy-looking creature who through the antelope's glazed eyes might have seemed antelope color. Snow everywhere around us but John's knee presses into rocky earth speckled here and there by subtle pinwheel explosions of lichen that cling to mountain turf you'd think would be lifeless buried years under snow and ice.

John snaps his pistol into its holster, slides the holster into a backpack on the ground next to the antelope, digs out of the pack a sheathed Bowie knife. When it's bare in his fist, I study it. One edge sharp as a razor, half the other edge beveled, saw-toothed. This is how I'll manage. Concentrate on the unfolding details of field-dressing an antelope. Focus my curiosity on each step without asking why or connecting the dots. Like watching a striptease. Or like enjoying Walt's Alibi tall tales, letting him have his fun at my expense, good ole Walt busting my balls, skinning me to entertain the others. Uh-huh. I hear you, Walt, but I'm not Roger. I can laugh as hard and invisibly inside myself as you laugh behind your poker face, old buddy.

That morning or another in the mountains I remember thinking about how love could make going to sleep each night a long journey, a long separation from the loved one, and how I'd say *I'll miss you* to her before turning away to my side of the bed. Remember being offered John's pistol and declining. Remember thinking here's this whole bloodthirsty bunch of us and just one skimpy antelope each guy probably outweighs. I remember a wounded animal stumbling and lurching like a drunk, remember being riveted by the unlikelihood of what I was witnessing, a wild creature approaching closer and closer, its body begging, speaking, if the word *speak* means anything, speaking the sentence *Please finish killing me.*

John's got the antelope's spindly hind legs lifted and splayed, gets rid of prick and balls, then wiggles the knife tip under the hide and slices slowly, carefully, from crotch to chest. Sounds like cutting carpet. No, fellas, I don't gasp when John opens the antelope's distended water-balloon belly and yanks out steaming viscera. I'm digging erotic pinks and vivid lavenders, delicate mauves of stretched, moist skin, the smell discharged with a palpable hiss, engulfing me, not in fetid nastiness of bile or vomit but sage perfume, so familiar, pungent, and intimate I've never forgotten it, and that nearly-falling-in-love swoon as close as I came that day to losing my composure.

I intended to return to this skinning and gutting scene, squeeze more out of it, but between one writing session and the next, while reading Haruki Murakami's *Wind-Up Bird Chronicle,* I encountered, by coincidence, another skinning scene — the torture of a Japanese soldier captured during the Manchurian border war between Russia and Japan in 1939, a graphic description of a man tied down and flayed inch by inch by a Mongolian with a long, thin, curved knife, who prolonged his victim's agony less to extract information than to demonstrate mastery of his instrument, which produced perfectly preserved, empty envelopes of skin while the bloody body still twitched.

Whatever little chill I hoped to evoke with my antelope butchering scene had been trumped and chumped by the horrible suffering of Murakami's prisoner, his human screams, human blood soaking the ground, the patient, methodical infliction of pain by his executioner. I felt depressed, disappointed, hopelessly outgunned. A tiny razor was lifting my skin.

Luckily, I had other work, so put Wyoming aside that day, tried to savor the irony of yet another coincidence and console myself with the possibility, whether I liked it or not, that coincidence was becoming my subject, the inevitable subject once you start searching for connections between one word and the next, one step and the next, one breath, one heartbeat, and the next, because sooner or later coincidence intervenes, a spinning universe intersects with another spinning universe, and strangely, one doesn't exactly demolish the other, each seems to go on about its business as if the other doesn't exist, the *bumping* into each other, the *touching* are fictions, imaginary accidents that produce consequences a survivor of the collision might call *change* or *loss* or *birth* or *death*.

Coincidence (1) the fact or condition of being coincidental, (2) occurrence or existence at the same time, (3) exact correspondence in substance, nature, character, etc., (4) concurrence, (5) blending.

And further down page 339 of the *Oxford Shorter English Dictionary* (Volume 1, A–M), where coincidentally my eyes stray,

> *Cohabit*—to dwell together
> *Coinquinate*—to soil all over; pollute; defile

Play in the dictionary all day, but you'll still never write like the great ones, the voice says. But so what, why should I. The point isn't replicating some other writer. The point is expressing myself, being myself. Anyway, who decides, finally, what's good or bad, and hearing myself repeat the pep talk I deliver each time a writer's shadow or my own ineptitude stops me in my tracks, I think, yeah, right, but how can I be sure my bones aren't up in the mountains already, waiting for some spring hiker to boot them deeper into a snowdrift.

Maybe what seems real is merely a possibility, never more, never more than one possibility among innumerable others. To imagine one life, we let go of others. Bury them like burying the dead. Until coincidence recalls them.

This morning when I took a break from writing I picked up *Tracing*, a book of poems that's been sitting around months unopened, and carried it into the bathroom to glance at while I sat on the toilet. I could say this book this morning a coincidence, or say I'm compelled to crack the book this particular morning because it's a gift from a nice person, because it's fragile-looking, probably self-printed, a gray paper cover thin as each of its twenty or so stapled-together pages, read it because writers are hunters, because the author of the poems, Ryoko Sekiguchi, coincidentally, is Japanese like Murakami. The first words of the first poem are *The unexpected meeting in the singular suddenly becomes numerous.*

When John phoned to say he'd be in the city the following week and maybe we could hang out, I almost laughed out loud. Only reason I didn't because too much to explain before John could appreciate the joke that wasn't really funny in the first place, more like bizarre, more like crazy, like poor Molly and her talking license plates. About three years since we'd hooked up, but with all the Wyoming stuff in the air, why not, why wouldn't my best friend from that time and place arrive on my doorstep. Why not one further funhouse-mirror twist — in addition to seeing me, John intended to catch up with other old friends, mutual friends from Wyoming in town for the same conference he's attending. Did I want to join the whole crew for dinner. He didn't say for old time's sake or say just like in the good ole days but what else would he be thinking, the coincidence of everybody in the same city, same day, the possibility of getting together again, nostalgia, reprieve, the bunch of us performing the neat trick of going back to a place that no longer exists or never existed. Who can resist. The innocent smiles, the hugs and chatter and toasts. My, my. I wanted to laugh out loud and cry and confess everything to my old pal. Explain why meeting would do no good. Why meetings scripted and unscripted, especially the latter, and it's always partly the latter, are as dangerous as they are sad and unforgiving, as they are fun and funny. I couldn't wait to see him. Yeah. Sure. I'll join him and kick back with the others. None of the dead need apply. Yes. Sounds great. After all, unbeknown to myself, I'd been preparing, hadn't I. Warming up. Practicing quick cuts from figure to ground, ground to figure. Like the design printed on my African gourd. Fish flying or birds swimming, or some new winged, amphibious hybrid, at home in water, earth, fire, wind, at home on the range.

How long will my old buddy wait in the hotel lobby, grinning as if he's enjoying the joke I haven't told him, appearing as pleased with himself as any aging magician who cups in his hands a live, wiggly baby rabbit plucked from an empty top hat, then claps to prove to the audience nothing in his hands after all.

I think I catch him catch a glimpse of me out of the corner of his eye. Swear I see the flicker of his glance light me up a minisecond and his long mouth begin a smile of recognition. I must be mistaken, because when his head turns and he gazes directly at the space I occupy, his glance, then his fixed stare, pass straight through me as if I'm not a few yards away, as if he's daydreaming or remembering a meeting elsewhere with someone else on some other occasion, or as if he's been tricked by some coincidental movement and turns to find no one there.